The price of fame . . .

"Elizabeth, you're doing fabulously," Marian shouted. "Jenny, if you're not sure about the combination, watch Elizabeth. Do what she does."

The unexpected praise sent a surge of adrenaline through Elizabeth's body. The music picked up, climbed to another key, and moved into the driving finale.

She imagined she was dancing in front of an enormous staircase, the set of a 1930s musical. She turned, prepared to dance up the grand staircase with her hat lifted, and then—

Splat!

One minute Elizabeth had been skimming over the highly polished floor like a bird over water. The next minute she was sliding across it facedown, like a hockey puck.

The piano music came to an abrupt halt.

"Elizabeth, what happened?" Marian asked.

"She tripped over her own foot," Jenny Pearman explained, gazing at her with sympathetic emerald green eyes—eyes that were just a little too sympathetic.

You tripped me, Elizabeth thought angrily as she glared at Jenny.

Visit the Official Sweet Valley Web Site on the Internet at:

http://www.sweetvalley.com

SWEET VALLEY TWINS

The Twins Hit Hollywood

Written by
Jamie Suzanne

Created by
FRANCINE PASCAL

BANTAM BOOKS
NEW YORK · TORONTO · LONDON · SYDNEY · AUCKLAND

To Randy Boulton

RL 4, 008-012

THE TWINS HIT HOLLYWOOD
A Bantam Book / June 1997

Sweet Valley High® and Sweet Valley Twins® are
registered trademarks of Francine Pascal.

Conceived by Francine Pascal.

Produced by Daniel Weiss Associates, Inc.
33 West 17th Street
New York, NY 10011.

Cover art by Bruce Emmett.

ISBN: 0-553-48438-9

Published simultaneously in the United States and Canada

Bantam Books are published by Bantam Books, a division of Bantam
Doubleday Dell Publishing Group, Inc. Its trademark, consisting of the
words "Bantam Books" and the portrayal of a rooster, is Registered in the
U.S. Patent and Trademark Office and in other countries. Marca
Registrada. Bantam Books, 1540 Broadway, New York, New York 10036.

PRINTED IN THE UNITED STATES OF AMERICA

OPM   0 9 8 7 6 5 4 3 2 1

One

◇

"Hey, Steven," Elizabeth Wakefield greeted her fourteen-year-old brother as she sat down across from him at the breakfast table.

Steven continued to shovel cereal into his mouth, his eyes glued to the comics page of the newspaper.

Elizabeth cleared her throat. "Good *morning!*" she prompted.

He grunted something that sounded vaguely like "good morning" without taking his eyes off the page.

Steven had never been a morning person, but Elizabeth thought he looked even glummer and more heavy-lidded than usual. Before she could ask him if something was wrong, the doorbell rang.

Elizabeth heard her identical twin sister, Jessica, run downstairs to answer it.

Steven reached for the Corny O's box and added more cereal to the milk in his bowl.

"Take it easy on those Corny O's," Elizabeth joked. "We've only got nineteen more boxes. We don't want to run out."

Steven made a face at his sister. "I'll try to control my appetite," he said, and turned back to the comics.

Elizabeth and Jessica had recently starred in a hugely successful commercial for the popular breakfast cereal. Part of their payment had been a lifetime supply of Corny O's.

Because of child labor laws, the production company wanted identical twins for the sixty-second spot so that they could take turns playing the same part.

Jessica and Elizabeth Wakefield were so identical, sometimes they couldn't even tell themselves apart in pictures. Each girl had large blue-green eyes, long blond hair, and a dimple in her left cheek. But their personalities were as different as night and day. While Jessica was flamboyant and impulsive, Elizabeth was more thoughtful and organized.

Unfortunately, their different personalities had resulted in drastically different artistic interpretations of the part. Each thought her own way was better, and there had been a few battles on the set of the Corny O's commercial. Luckily, however, the director had been able to cut the film he'd taken during their very worst fight so that in the final version the twins appeared to be one daredevil twelve-year-old.

It hadn't been *fun*, exactly, Elizabeth decided as

she thought back on the Corny O's commercial, but she was glad they had done it. Their parents had made them put most of the money away for college, but she'd had enough left over to buy a desktop publishing system for the *Sweet Valley Sixers*, the Sweet Valley Middle School newspaper that she edited with her friend Amy Sutton. And all their friends had seen the commercial and thought it was totally cool.

Elizabeth was just reaching for the cereal box when she heard an earsplitting scream from the front hall. Instantly she jumped out of her seat and ran toward the hall, with Steven right behind her.

Mr. Wakefield came running into the kitchen, shaving cream covering half his face and smeared on his bathrobe. "What's wrong? Who screamed? What's the matter?"

Mrs. Wakefield ran in behind him. She was dressed in tailored pants, a silk shirt, and a blazer, but her hair was still wet.

Jessica's face was as white as a sheet. Her mouth opened and closed as if she were in shock. In her hand was a piece of paper, which she shook in Elizabeth's face.

Elizabeth snatched the paper from Jessica's hand. It was a letter, and as she skimmed it she could hardly believe what she was reading. When she reached the bottom of the letter, she opened her mouth and let out a scream herself. It was the only appropriate response.

Steven covered his ears with his hands. "Good grief!"

"Girls!" Mrs. Wakefield exclaimed in an alarmed tone. "Will you please tell us what's going on?"

Elizabeth looked at her parents, her face shining. "Remember that talent scout, Paul Tremont, who called us after seeing the Corny O's commercial? Well, he recommended us to a company called Star Quality Casting. This letter says they want us to audition for parts in a movie—'a major motion picture,' it says!"

"Oh, honey, that's wonderful!" Mrs. Wakefield exclaimed, and Mr. Wakefield grinned broadly.

But Steven clutched his head. "Oh, no!" he groaned. "Here we go again!"

Half an hour later Steven stood in the front hall waiting for Jessica and Elizabeth. All the excitement had put the family about twenty minutes behind schedule, so Mrs. Wakefield was going to drive everybody to school on her way to a meeting with a client.

Steven shoved some tissues into the pocket of his jeans. The twins had had a cold last week. Now he felt as if he was coming down with it.

He considered telling his mother he didn't feel well enough to go to school. He wouldn't mind spending the day in front of the TV with a big pitcher of orange juice. But if he told her he was sick, she might not let him go to basketball practice the next afternoon. Steven was on the Sweet Valley High basketball team, and there was no way he wanted to miss practice. There was a big game coming up in a couple of weeks, and he had to be at the top of his game.

Steven grabbed his jacket from the rack in the hallway, deciding to keep his mouth shut.

"Steven, dahling!" drawled a voice from the top of the stairs.

Steven turned and saw Jessica striking a dramatic pose. Her hair was piled high on her head, she wore a pair of cat's-eye-shaped rhinestone-studded sunglasses, and her feet wobbled on high-heeled sandals.

Steven snorted. He didn't know much about fashion, but he had a feeling their mother's high heels didn't exactly go with Jessica's jeans and purple T-shirt.

"What's so funny?" Mrs. Wakefield stepped into the hallway, her briefcase in her hand. When she saw Jessica, she raised an eyebrow. "All right, young lady! Are you going to cooperate, or do I have to call the fashion police?"

"Mom!" Jessica protested. "This is exactly the kind of outfit Connie Boyer wears."

"Connie Boyer isn't a sixth-grader at Sweet Valley Middle School," Mrs. Wakefield pointed out.

A well-known TV and film star, Connie Boyer was famous for being glamorous, but she was also notorious for being outrageously rude and obnoxious. Unfortunately Jessica seemed to have picked her for her latest role model.

"Lose the high heels and the big hair," Mrs. Wakefield told Jessica. "You can keep the sunglasses. That's my best offer."

"I'd lose the sunglasses too, Jess," Steven added with a smirk. "They make you look like a dork."

Jessica sighed and sat down on the steps. "OK, OK. I had a feeling this might happen." She kicked off the shoes and pulled some sneakers from her backpack, then removed a few pins from her hair and shook it out. She lifted the rhinestone sunglasses briefly to glare at her brother, then lowered them into place again, remarking, "*Some* people in this family have no taste."

Elizabeth came downstairs with her backpack and stopped when she saw Jessica. "Are you wearing those sunglasses to school?" she asked.

"Yes, I am," Jessica said defiantly. "Why not?"

"Because you look silly," Elizabeth answered in a reasonable tone.

"Silly?" Jessica gasped.

Steven snorted.

"Shut *up*," she hissed at him. Then she turned to her sister. "Elizabeth! Don't you have *any* fashion sense? These are exactly like the glasses that Connie Boyer wore during her guest appearance on *Red Oak Apartments* where she tells Brad Belmontaine that she can't marry him because she's really a spy."

"I don't care," Elizabeth said stubbornly. "You look ridiculous."

Jessica defiantly pushed the glasses up the

bridge of her nose and swept past Elizabeth with her chin up. "Well! You're entitled to your opinion. And I'm entitled to mine."

Elizabeth rolled her eyes and followed Jessica out of the house. "Excuse *me!*"

"Girls," Mrs. Wakefield scolded, turning to lock the front door, "please! I don't want to have to listen to you bicker this early in the morning."

"Like I said," Steven said gloomily, "here we go again."

"You're going to be in a real movie?" Mandy Miller breathed. "Not just a commercial?"

Jessica pushed her sunglasses up on her nose. "Please, Mandy," she drawled. "Get the lingo right. It's not a *movie*. It's a *major motion picture*. And Elizabeth and I won't be playing the same part, like we did in the commercial. The movie is about a set of identical twins and their older sister, and there's a part for each of us."

Jessica removed her sandwich from her lunch bag and made a mental note to buy a small wicker picnic basket to carry her lunch in—and a new leather backpack to carry the basket in. She'd never seen a picture of any important movie star carrying a tuna fish sandwich in a brown paper bag stuffed inside a ratty old nylon backpack.

Jessica and her friends were sitting at the Unicorner, their customary table in the Sweet Valley Middle School cafeteria. The Unicorns were a group of girls who considered themselves the prettiest and most popular at Sweet Valley Middle School. Elizabeth had been asked to join, but she had dropped out after two meetings because she thought the girls were silly and snobby. But Jessica loved being part of the in crowd. And more than anything else, she loved being the center of the in crowd's attention.

"You are soooo lucky!" Tamara Chase said in an envious voice. "I'd give anything to be in a movie."

"She's not in the movie yet," Lila Fowler snapped. "So if I were you, Jessica, I wouldn't get too carried away."

Jessica smirked. Lila was her best friend, but the two girls were very competitive. Most of the time Lila came out on top, mainly because she was one of the richest girls in California and made sure that everyone knew it. If Jessica bought a new sweater, Lila would buy six expensive tops, three skirts, and two pairs of shoes. If Jessica got a CD player for Christmas, Lila would get her father to buy her a home entertainment center with a fifty-inch television screen. If Jessica's family went to the amusement park, Lila would talk her dad into vacationing in Europe.

It really got on Jessica's nerves sometimes. But now that Jessica had finally found a way to outdo Lila, naturally Lila was trying to rain all over her parade.

Jessica remembered an interview she had watched featuring Connie Boyer. "You don't have any friends in this business," Connie had said in her trademark sneer. "And that's OK with me, because as far as I'm concerned, friends are just dead weight."

Connie Boyer knew what she was talking about, Jessica thought. Lila would never be any help to her, but she was glad Lila was her friend anyway. It was going to be *so* much fun showing her up.

She and Elizabeth would get that part. By spring vacation she would own her own Beverly Hills mansion. Then she would invite all the Unicorns over to meet her Hollywood friends—all the Unicorns *except Lila!*

"What's with Jessica and the weird sunglasses?" Amy Sutton asked Elizabeth at lunch.

"I was wondering the same thing," Maria Hughes said. "She wore them all during English. I doubt she could see anything the teacher wrote on the board."

Elizabeth looked over at the Unicorner. When her sister lowered the hot dog she was eating, Elizabeth could see she was indeed wearing her cat's-eye sunglasses—and a large streak of mustard on her cheek. Elizabeth giggled. Jessica looked pretty silly.

"Well, I wasn't going to tell you guys just yet, but since I'm sure Jessica is telling anybody who'll listen . . ." Elizabeth took a bite of her bologna sandwich and smiled. "We got a letter from Star Quality Casting inviting us to audition for a movie."

"No *way!*" Amy gasped.

Maria's eyes widened, and she let out a low whistle. "Star Quality is one of the biggest casting companies in Hollywood. They cast most of the big-budget movies." Maria had been a child actress in Hollywood a few years before, so she knew a lot about the movie business.

"It's just an audition," Elizabeth reminded her. "It doesn't mean we have the part or anything."

"I'm *sure* you'll get the part," Amy said. "And then the *Sixers* can run an exclusive interview with the hottest new stars in show business."

Elizabeth and Maria laughed. "Think positive," Maria said. "They wouldn't have asked you to audition if they thought you really weren't right."

Elizabeth looked over at Jessica again. Her sister was tossing her head around as if she were a model on a photo shoot. "I guess," Elizabeth responded with a sigh.

"You don't sound too happy about it," Maria said.

"Well, I'm sure it'll be fun, but I'm a little worried about Jessica. She gets so carried away with this kind of stuff."

"You mean the sunglasses?" Amy asked.

Elizabeth nodded. "I guess I'm worried about myself too."

Maria took a sip of milk. "How so?"

Elizabeth nervously crumpled the edge of her napkin. "When we did that Corny O's commercial, I started acting just as crazy as Jessica. Maria, you're always saying that show business brings out the worst in people. I'm just worried that it'll change me, whether I like it or not."

Amy laughed. "Look at it this way. Whatever you did during the Corny O's commercial, it worked. It was a great commercial. Besides, you're the most down-to-earth person we know."

Maria nodded. "The nicest too. All the movie roles in the world couldn't change that."

"I hope so," Elizabeth answered.

A brittle, actressy laugh floated toward them from the Unicorner. "Ah-*hah*-heh-heh-heh!" Jessica sounded amused and evil at the same time.

"Why is Jessica laughing like a mad scientist from a horror movie?" Amy asked.

"I think she's trying to laugh like Connie Boyer," Maria chuckled. "And she's doing a pretty good job! Connie Boyer *sounds* like a mad scientist in a horror movie—which is maybe why she's been in so many horror movies."

Elizabeth smiled at Maria's joke, but as Jessica continued to laugh she felt a nervous flutter in her stomach. Elizabeth knew that the slightest whiff of show business turned her sister into a lunatic who would stop at nothing to get a part. She would take any chance, use any trick. It was actually kind of scary.

And the scariest part, Elizabeth thought, was that Jessica's lunacy seemed to be contagious.

Two

◇

"Stop!" Jessica shouted.

Mr. Wakefield jammed his foot on the brake, and Elizabeth lurched forward. "Oof!" she grunted as her seat belt dug into her stomach.

"What? What?" Mr. Wakefield asked, looking in every direction.

Elizabeth peered through the window, expecting to see an eighteen-wheeler bearing down on them. But all she saw were a few pedestrians darting between the cars and vans. They were driving through a part of Los Angeles in which old warehouses had been converted to residential lofts, art galleries, and rehearsal spaces.

"This is the place!" Jessica said eagerly. She pointed to the number over the door of a large loft building. "The letter says to go to the rehearsal studio on the fourth floor."

Mr. Wakefield pulled over to the curb, and Jessica slid open the side door of the minivan and jumped out before the car had come to a stop. "Jessica!" Mr. Wakefield scolded sharply. "That's dangerous. Be careful."

But Jessica was too busy touching up her makeup in the side mirror to respond.

Mr. Wakefield sighed and looked at Elizabeth. "Please keep an eye on your sister," he told her.

"I'll try," Elizabeth said with a laugh. She had been nervous all day. It was hard to anticipate what kind of nutty thing Jessica might do.

Elizabeth kissed her dad's cheek and climbed out. "I don't know how long this will take, so we'll take the bus home."

"If it's dark, though, call and I'll pick you up." Mr. Wakefield grinned and gave the twins a thumbs-up. "Knock 'em dead," he said before rolling up the window and pulling away from the curb.

"Here," Jessica said, handing Elizabeth her lip gloss. "Better use mine so we're both wearing the same shade."

"Good idea." Elizabeth rolled the light pink lip gloss over her lips.

Jessica plunged her hand deep into her backpack and fished out another pair of rhinestone-studded cat's-eye sunglasses. "And take these," she said, thrusting them at Elizabeth.

"What are those for?"

"They're for you. We're supposed to look alike," Jessica reminded her.

Elizabeth took a deep breath. She might as well nip this thing in the bud. "Forget it, Jess."

"Elizabeth!"

"I am not wearing those stupid-looking sunglasses," Elizabeth insisted.

"They are *not* stupid-looking!" Jessica argued. "I spent my own money to get these for you. I saw them advertised in a magazine: 'The Connie Boyer style—as seen on TV.'" Seeing that this wasn't going to change her twin's mind, she repeated in a whine, "But we're supposed to look alike."

"I don't care," Elizabeth said stubbornly. "I let you talk me into spraying my hair into a flip. I let you talk me into wearing these bell-bottom pants. And I let you talk me into wearing glitter laces in my tennis shoes. But I'm not wearing those sunglasses."

Jessica sighed and dropped the glasses back in her backpack. "OK. You win." She pulled her own sunglasses off and dropped them in the backpack too.

Elizabeth smiled. *So Jessica is capable of being reasonable. All I have to do is be firm.*

Then Jessica reached into her backpack and removed a little plastic box. Very carefully she snapped open the lid and gingerly removed something. "Since you won't wear the sunglasses . . . here!" She dangled something hairy in front of Elizabeth's face.

Elizabeth's heart missed a beat. *A tarantula!* "Are you crazy?" she screamed. She lifted her own backpack and swatted the hairy spider from Jessica's fingers. *Did I say my sister could be reasonable? Scratch that—she's insane!*

The tarantula fell on the sidewalk, and Elizabeth stomped on it . . . again . . . and again . . . and again . . .

Jessica grabbed her arm. "Elizabeth! Elizabeth! Get a grip! What's with you?"

Elizabeth stopped stomping. Breathing heavily, she turned on Jessica. "What are you trying to do?" she screamed. "Kill me just because I wouldn't wear your stupid sunglasses?"

"Well, *excuse* me," Jessica said, staring at her as if she had lost her mind. "I didn't realize that you were going to react so negatively to every little beauty tip."

Every little beauty tip? Elizabeth gingerly removed her foot and looked down at the pavement. She had just killed . . . a false eyelash!

Jessica shook her head. "Gosh, Elizabeth. It's really scary how far you'll go to get your own way on stuff like this. When we get inside, please try not to do anything that would embarrass me."

Jessica leaned over and gave her hair one final volume-building shake as the elevator climbed to the fourth floor.

Would any of the stars of the movie be there to watch her audition? Or would it be just the director? She could just imagine the conversation between the Star Quality Casting agent and the director of the movie.

The agent swiveled around in his chair and put his feet up on the desk. He puffed a big cigar as he said into the phone, "Guess what? We actually managed to get the Wakefield twins."

On the other end of the line, a handsome young director sat by a swimming pool, speaking on a cellular phone. "You mean the girls in the Corny O's commercial?"

"That's right," the casting agent said. "We're bringing them in for an audition. But it's a formality. Let's face it, there aren't many sets of identical twins with talent like that. They're one in a million. Or should I say two in a million? Ha ha ha ha ha."

As the elevator doors opened on the fourth floor, Jessica lifted her chin and plastered a huge smile across her face.

But no casting agent or director stood there waiting to greet her. All she saw were twins. Directly to their right was a set of identical twin girls with short red curly hair and big blue eyes. They wore green shorts, green striped T-shirts, and green tennis shoes with green-and-white striped socks.

The room was filled with twins—tall ones, short ones, fat ones, and skinny ones.

Jessica shook her head. "I can't believe it. There's two of everybody."

She and Elizabeth edged their way over to the registration desk, where a man wearing a baseball cap and a navy blue blazer seemed to be checking people in.

Jessica and Elizabeth found a spot in the clump of people that was supposed to be the line.

"This is a lot of competition," Elizabeth remarked.

Jessica studied the redheads. She nudged Elizabeth. "Actually, if you look at their faces and not their matching hair and green outfits, they don't look that much alike."

Behind her, a girl with her dark hair in pigtails sniffed. "Fraternal," she commented disdainfully. She smiled at Jessica. "I'm Louise Parker. And this is my sister, Tammy."

Tammy smiled. "Hi!"

"I'm Jessica and this is Elizabeth," Jessica said.

"Wow!" Tammy said. "You two are totally identical. Can your friends tell you apart?"

"Not unless we want them to," Jessica said proudly. "You two are really identical too."

Louise preened a little. "Thanks."

"So have you guys tried out for things before?" Jessica asked.

"We've been on the twin circuit for a long time," Louise answered. "Tammy and I have made at least twenty commercials since we started."

"At age five," Tammy interjected.

Louise nodded. "And we've appeared on the *Jim Winger Show, Kid to Kid*, and tons of TV movies."

"Wow!" Elizabeth said. "You guys are real professionals."

"Oh, yeah," Louise confirmed. "We're definitely professional. And we see a lot of the same people over and over." She nodded toward the redheaded girls. "Like those two. I don't know why the fraternals always show up for these things. They're not fooling anybody."

"There are a lot of people here who shouldn't be," Tammy whispered. "Look. See those girls with the blond bangs? They're not even the same height."

Jessica studied them closely. Tammy was right. One twin was a good two inches taller than the other.

"This audition is for twins between ten and thirteen. Those African American girls in the braids aren't a day over nine," Tammy continued. Her eyes flickered over the crowd and her lips moved as she counted softly. "One . . . two . . . *three* pairs of twins are different weights. And those girls in the corner? Don't *tell* me they're not over the age limit."

Jessica squinted, studying the crowd. Tammy was right—a lot of the others didn't belong there. Once you eliminated the fraternal pairs and the ones that were too old or too young, the competition thinned out. She began to feel more optimistic.

"Have you two ever auditioned for Star Quality before?" Louise asked as the line moved forward.

Elizabeth shook her head. "No. What about you guys?"

Louise shook her head. "No. Most of the stuff we've done was in New York. We just moved to California a few months ago."

Jessica and Elizabeth were now at the registration desk. "Hi!" The man in the baseball cap and blazer gave them a friendly smile. "I'm Jack. Who are you?"

"Jessica and Elizabeth Wakefield," Jessica said. "Stars of the Corny O's commercial," she added in a louder voice. She wanted to make sure that

Louise and Tammy didn't get the impression that she and Elizabeth didn't belong here either.

"I saw that commercial," Jack said. "Nice work."

"Thank you," Jessica and Elizabeth replied at the same time.

"Can you tell us anything about the movie?" Jessica asked eagerly. "What it's about, and who's going to be in it?"

The man shook his head. "We're just a casting company. We're not authorized to give out any information about the project. If you're chosen, the production company will fill you in." He smiled. "Sorry. But that's show biz. Everything's top secret at the beginning."

Jessica felt her heart thump. Just hearing somebody use words such as *casting, production,* and *secret* was exciting.

The man checked off their names on a list and handed them each a clipboard. "Fill out these forms, please, and place them on that table over there. Then just take a seat and wait. That's the downside of show biz," he said with a laugh. "It's always hurry up and wait."

Jessica grinned, took one clipboard, and handed the other to Elizabeth. She couldn't resist smirking at Louise and Tammy as they moved up to the desk. The man was familiar with their work. And he'd complimented them. She and Elizabeth had an edge.

As they passed the redheaded twins, Jessica gave them a long and contemptuous look. *Poor things,* she thought. It was really kind of pathetic the way they tried to pretend to be identical. She gazed at Elizabeth with new appreciation. Elizabeth could look like Jessica without even trying.

"How long have we been here?" Jessica asked for about the fiftieth time.

"The same length of time as the last time you asked. About two hours," Elizabeth answered.

"What are they *doing*?" Jessica asked impatiently.

"How should I know?" Elizabeth snapped. The prospect of being in a movie had been exciting—two hours earlier. But sitting around waiting with a huge crowd of other hopefuls without even a book to read was mind-numbingly boring. She was beginning to be sorry that she and Jessica had agreed to do this.

Like Jessica, Elizabeth had expected to walk in and be greeted personally by someone who knew them by name. She'd pictured drinking a little juice, answering a few questions, and maybe even reciting a few lines from *Romeo and Juliet*. She'd never expected to have to sit for hours in the middle of a mob scene, much less one that was wall-to-wall twins.

All the adults associated with the casting company had disappeared into an inner office with the forms the twins had filled out. No one had emerged to give them an update or even tell them when they could expect to audition.

For the first hour, people had eagerly mixed and mingled. Elizabeth had met a lot of nice kids. Some of them had really interesting stories to tell. She thought it would be fun to interview them for the *Sixers*.

But after the first hour the suspense had begun to take its toll. People began to look more and more nervous. Now there was very little conversation, and no laughter at all.

The twin who was growing out her perm chewed nervously at her thumbnail. The red-headed twins looked tired and a little drawn.

Tammy and Louise didn't look worried at all. They were pretty cool customers—probably because they had been through lots of auditions before, Elizabeth figured.

A door opened. Jessica was the first person in the hallway to jump to her feet. She yanked Elizabeth's arm, and Elizabeth scrambled up along with everyone else when Jack came out with a list in his hand. He lifted the baseball cap and scratched his head before settling the cap more firmly over his brow. "First of all, I want to thank everyone for coming. We know you went to a lot of trouble, and we appreciate it. Most of you have some show business experience, so I hope you won't take it personally if we've eliminated you. I'd like the following twins to come back tomorrow and work with us a little longer." He lifted the clipboard. "Jenny and Tricia Pearman . . ."

Two girls to Elizabeth's right grinned and high-fived each other. Elizabeth had figured they would get picked. She'd never seen two more beautiful girls. It was their eyes that were so incredible. They were a deep, clear emerald green.

". . . Raquel and Casey Carver . . ."

Two girls with shiny brown hair pumped their fists in the air. "All right!"

Elizabeth held her breath as Jack read out more names from his list. "Wakefield!" she heard Jessica urge in a whisper. "Say 'Wakefield.'"

". . . Louise and Tammy Parker . . ."

Louise and Tammy hugged each other.

". . . and Jessica and Elizabeth Wakefield."

Elizabeth's stomach lurched.

Jessica's hand clutched at her arm. "We made it through the first cut," she whispered joyously.

"Would the twins whose names I've just called please come inside the rehearsal studio?" Jack requested. "Everybody else, many thanks and good luck. Star Quality hopes we'll see you again soon."

Several dejected and muttering pairs of twins began leaving by the stairs. Some waited for the elevator.

Elizabeth and Jessica, Tammy and Louise, and eight other pairs of twins passed through the large, heavy door and walked into a big rehearsal studio.

Two walls were covered with mirrors. A wooden barre ran the length of each wall. The highly polished hardwood floor was as smooth as glass. A piano stood in the corner.

Two women with bright blond hair sat at a table with piles of application forms. They were dressed almost exactly alike in tight black pants and form-fitting animal-print blouses.

The older of the two women sorted through some papers, then came over to address the group. "Girls, I'm Marian Willis, the president of Star Quality Casting, and these are my assistants, Jack Hernandez and Shirley Bonham. Over the next few days we're going to be looking at your singing, dancing, and dramatic abilities. We'll be shooting test film as well. I want everybody to work hard, but let's keep our perspective, OK? It's just a movie."

"Just a movie?" Jessica whispered to Elizabeth. "More like just our whole life. This is the start of something big. I can feel it."

Elizabeth felt a shudder of excitement run through her body. Boredom, fear, and doubt were forgotten. She and Jessica just might get starring roles in a major motion picture.

It *did* feel like the start of something big.

The remaining twins began to eye each other.

Elizabeth realized with a shock that Tammy was staring right at her. Elizabeth smiled.

Tammy smiled back, but only from the nose down. Her eyes looked hard, flat, and cold. Louise's eyes had that same look as she surveyed the crowd.

Elizabeth shuddered involuntarily.

Apparently it felt like the start of something big to *everybody*, including Tammy and Louise.

Three

"Come on," Jessica said as they left the building. "The bus won't be here for another twenty minutes. Let's get a soda while we wait." She pointed to a small café across the street, where several of the twin finalists were going in.

"Good idea," Elizabeth agreed. All that audition drama had made her thirsty. They crossed the street and hurried into the café.

Elizabeth looked around. The only famous faces she saw were on the wall, where there were rows of autographed head shots.

"There's Connie Boyer!" Jessica hurried over to the wall to examine the picture.

One of the twin finalists, a girl with short dark hair, sidled over to Jessica. "Look at that one down there," she said, pointing to another photo.

When Jessica leaned over to get a better look, Elizabeth saw that the girl was holding a long, gleaming pair of scissors behind her back.

That's strange, Elizabeth thought. *What is she doing with those—* Suddenly Elizabeth realized exactly what the girl was doing. "Jessica! Look out!" she shouted.

Jessica straightened up just as the girl was about to cut a large chunk out of her hair. The girl immediately hid the scissors behind her back again.

Jessica turned toward Elizabeth. "What's the matter?" she asked.

Elizabeth's mouth opened and closed. She was so stunned, she could hardly find the words to tell Jessica how close she'd come to getting an unauthorized haircut.

Two girl twins with long dark hair to their waist walked by, laughing and giggling.

The girl with the scissors reached out and—*snip!*—cut off a huge hunk of one of the twins' hair.

Elizabeth gasped. The girl whose hair had been shorn let out an outraged howl. She turned toward the girl with the scissors. "Chrissy Peterson, you are a fink. I'm going to tell Equity about this!" Then she burst into tears.

Her identical twin reached over and picked the hair off the floor, gazing at it sadly.

Jessica hurried back over to Elizabeth's side. Instinctively they reached for each other's hand and backed away from the scene in horror.

"Watch out!" a voice cautioned.

Elizabeth and Jessica both screamed and whirled around, holding their hands over their hair.

Louise and Tammy stood behind them.

"Did you see what happened?" Elizabeth whispered.

Tammy sipped her milk shake as if nothing very important had taken place.

Louise laughed nastily. "Oldest trick in the show biz twin book. Penny and Polly Gilbert beat out the Peterson girls for six hair care commercials in a row. I think their winning streak is over now."

Elizabeth couldn't believe it. "How can you laugh?" she demanded.

Louise shrugged. "Hey, all's fair in love, war, and the movie business. The casting agents want twins that look alike. Penny and Polly don't look alike anymore—unless Penny wants to cut off her hair too. And I don't think that's going to happen. Her hair is so long she can sit on it. It's worth a fortune in shampoo and conditioner commercials."

"Let's get out of here," Elizabeth said to Jessica in a shaky voice.

For once Jessica didn't argue.

"I'm quitting," Elizabeth announced on the bus as Jessica slid into the seat beside her.

"Why?" Jessica cried.

"Because I'm scared."

"Of the Peterson twins? Nobody would try something like that twice. We'll just wear our hair in tight buns from now on. And make sure we know who's behind us."

Elizabeth sighed. "I mean I'm scared we might turn into people like that."

"Like the Peterson twins?" Jessica widened her eyes. "Somehow, Lizzie, I just don't see you walking around with scissors."

"No," Elizabeth said, her voice breaking. "I don't think I'd ever sink as low as the Petersons. I'm more worried I'd wind up like the Parker twins. Or the Gianelli twins. The Peterson twins are bad, but the Parkers are worse. They thought it was *funny*. They don't care about other people's feelings at all. They don't care about anything but getting the part."

"Those people are show business professionals," Jessica argued. "They're tough. They're like Connie Boyer."

"They're horrible," Elizabeth said. "I'm not going back, and that's that."

"You're the most selfish person in the whole world." Jessica said.

"I am not!" Elizabeth shot back. "Now can we please drop it?"

"In your dreams," Steven muttered.

Elizabeth, Steven, and Jessica were all in the living room after dinner. Steven lay on the living room sofa reading a novel for his English class. Elizabeth was working on a large map project. She was trying to fill in the world's rivers, mountains, and borders. But it was hard to concentrate with Jessica begging, pleading, and wheedling. She was driving Elizabeth slightly crazy.

"Don't you care about me at all?" Jessica demanded, sitting down beside her.

"Jessica, please! I'm trying to fill in Eastern Europe." Elizabeth's fingers hovered over her box of colored pencils as she deliberated over what color to make the Czech Republic.

"The biggest opportunity of my whole life—*our* whole life—and you're going to ruin it for me." Jessica let her head fall onto the coffee table with a thump, right on top of Africa. Steven turned the page of his novel. "She's going to win, Elizabeth," he said. "You know she is. Why don't you just make it easy on yourself and give up now?"

Elizabeth laughed and began to sketch. "Not this time."

"Ha!" Steven answered.

"If I could do it without you, I would," Jessica said. "But I can't." She lifted her head, and Elizabeth anxiously checked her map for signs of pink blush. Then she looked at Jessica to make sure there was no green colored pencil on her sister.

Uh-oh!

Jessica's lip was trembling.

"Don't cry," Elizabeth begged.

"You're sunk," Steven said.

Jessica's large eyes filled with tears.

Elizabeth groaned. Here it came . . . creeping guilt. How did Jessica manage to do it?

"Never mind," Jessica said with a sniff. "Don't worry about it. Sure, it's a once-in-a-lifetime opportunity, but I'll get over it. I'll . . . I'll . . ." Tears streamed down Jessica's cheeks. Her hand groped for the box of tissues that usually sat on the table beside the sofa.

Steven had it on his chest. Without looking up from his book, he pulled a tissue from the box and held it out to Jessica.

Jessica snatched the tissue from his hand and loudly blew her nose. "I'll be completely humiliated. My friends will ridicule me. The Peterson twins will get the part. Bad people will win because *you* don't have the guts to stay in there and fight, but . . ."

"OK, OK, *OK!*" Elizabeth yelled. "Enough already. You win. I'll go back tomorrow. We'll probably get cut, though. And after that, I don't want to hear one more word about show business. *Ever!* Got it?"

Jessica beamed through her tears. "It's a deal. If we get cut tomorrow, you'll never hear another word about show business from me."

"In your dreams," Steven muttered again.

Four

"Are we late?" Elizabeth whispered when they arrived at the studio the next day after school.

Jessica looked around the rehearsal hall. Several pairs of twins were already assembled. All of them wore workout or dance clothes. Most of them stood at the barre, stretching. "No," Jessica whispered back. "I guess everybody's trying to make a good impression by showing up early. Come on. Let's stretch."

Jessica dropped her bag in the corner and took off her windbreaker and jeans. So did Elizabeth. They had been told to be prepared to dance, so they had worn matching blue and black diamond-pattern leotards, blue tights with coordinating slouch socks, and black jazz shoes.

Both girls wore their hair in tight buns.

They'd pinned little blue crocheted nets over them too—just to be on the safe side.

Elizabeth sat down on the floor to stretch, and Jessica went to the barre. She put one hand on the wooden rod, checked her posture in the mirror, and extended her leg. Curving one arm over her head, she leaned over her leg as gracefully as she could.

"Good move," said someone behind her.

"Yeow!" Jessica's hand flew protectively to the back of her head. She whirled around.

Tammy and Louise giggled. The Parker twins both wore their hair in tight coils on the sides of their head, with pink yarn ribbons. They wore bright pink sweatshirts, pink tights, and lavender athletic shorts. One sweatshirt had "Tammy" embroidered on the front. The other twin's sweatshirt said "Louise."

"Sorry to startle you," Louise said.

"That's OK," Jessica said, her heart slowing. Then she recalled what they'd said to her: "Good move." Her heart resumed its rapid beating again. Tammy and Louise were show business professionals, and they were complimenting her dancing. Jessica tried not to sound as pleased as she felt. "Well," she began nonchalantly, "my leg extension isn't *really* up to par today, but thanks."

Tammy snickered. "I wasn't talking about your dancing. I was talking about your hairdo. Better safe than sorry."

Jessica looked over at Elizabeth. She hoped Elizabeth wasn't overhearing this conversation.

The Parker girls sounded pretty nasty—as if they thought it was funny that the competition was so ferocious that Jessica had to protect her hair.

Fortunately Elizabeth was sitting on the floor with her legs stretched out in front of her, trying to touch her toes.

The door to the rehearsal hall swung open, and in walked the Peterson twins. "Will anything happen to them?" Jessica whispered. "I mean, won't Star Quality disqualify them or something?"

"Are you kidding?" Louise rolled her eyes, as though she couldn't believe how naive Jessica was. "You're supposed to look out for yourself in this business."

The door opened again, and Tammy gasped. "Look!"

Polly Gilbert walked in with her head held high. Her butchered hair had been recut and shaped into an attractive short style. She threw a resentful and defiant glance at the Peterson twins.

"What's she doing here?" Louise whispered. "She and her sister aren't identical anymore."

At that moment Penny walked in. She had the same haircut!

The room rustled with murmurs and whispers.

"That's unbelievable," Tammy whispered. "Penny actually cut her hair so they could continue with this audition! Do you realize how many shampoo commercials she gave up by cutting her hair?"

"You know what this means, don't you?" Louise said.

"No," Jessica said. "What does it mean?"

Louise narrowed her eyes. "It means they must know something we don't know. And they know that whatever we're auditioning for, it must be the role of the century."

The rehearsal pianist launched into a medley of some of Elizabeth's favorite Broadway show tunes. They had spent an hour and a half learning the dance combination, and now they were finally dancing. For the first time all afternoon, Elizabeth began to have fun.

Jessica was on Elizabeth's left. Jenny and Tricia Pearman, the green-eyed twins, were on Elizabeth's right.

Shirley was in front of the twenty kids, leading them through the combination, while Marian and Jack watched.

"Step . . . step . . . kick and step," Shirley shouted. "Back, two, three, four . . . front, two, three, four . . . kick . . . kick . . . and turn and . . ."

"Nancy!" Marian shouted from her perch. "Keep that leg straight. Jenny, you don't have the combination. Pay attention to what you're doing . . . that's better. Louise, flex your foot, don't point. Flex. Flex! Elizabeth . . ."

Elizabeth's heart sank. What was she doing wrong?

"Elizabeth, you're doing fabulously," Marian shouted. "You look great. Jenny, if you're not sure about the combination, watch Elizabeth. Do what she does."

The unexpected praise sent a surge of adrenaline

through Elizabeth's body. She could feel Jenny's eyes on her. She could feel *everybody's* eyes on her. It was incredibly exciting.

She pictured herself as the lead dancer in an old 1930s musical. She wore a top hat, a tuxedo coat, and high heels.

She imagined there was an elaborately draped, shimmering gold curtain behind her. The curtain went up and revealed an enormous staircase. Chorus girls fell into step beside her. She turned, prepared to dance up the grand staircase with her hat lifted, and then—

Splat!

One minute Elizabeth had been skimming over the highly polished floor like a bird over water. The next minute she was sliding across it facedown, like a hockey puck.

One of the Carver girls managed to jump out of the way in time. Her twin sister wasn't fast enough. Elizabeth knocked her and the rest of the second row over like bowling pins.

The piano music came to an abrupt halt.

She heard tennis shoes squeaking on the floor as the adults ran to assist. Jack and Shirley leaned over and helped Elizabeth to her feet. Marian inspected the face of the fallen Carver twin, then turned to Elizabeth. "Elizabeth, what happened?" she asked.

"She tripped over her own foot," Jenny Pearman explained.

Jenny's twin, Tricia, put her hand on Elizabeth's

arm. "Poor thing. What a fall! Are you all right?"

Elizabeth brushed herself off and tested her legs to be sure she hadn't pulled any muscles. Jenny Pearman gazed at her with sympathetic emerald green eyes— eyes that were just a little *too* sympathetic.

You tripped me, Elizabeth thought angrily as she glared at Jenny.

A smile hovered at the corner of Tricia's mouth.

And you know she tripped me, Elizabeth added mentally, shifting her gaze to Tricia.

But Elizabeth said nothing. What could she say? She didn't have any proof. "I guess I wasn't looking," she mumbled.

"You're probably tired. Let's take a break," Marian said.

"She *what?*" Jessica shouted.

"Shhh!" Elizabeth warned.

Jessica looked around to be sure no one was listening. They were standing near the soda machine in the hall. Most of the other twins were in the rest room. A few had gone back into the rehearsal hall to practice the combination. "Are you sure?" she asked Elizabeth. "I mean, you're not just getting paranoid after what happened yesterday?"

Elizabeth tilted her head back and took another big gulp of her soda before handing it to Jessica. "Jenny Pearman tripped me on purpose. I know it, she knows it, and her sister knows it."

Jessica took a swig. "Now I know it too." Her

eyes narrowed dangerously. "There's only one thing to do: trip them back. You take Jenny. I'll get Tricia."

"No," Elizabeth said. "We're not going to sink to their level."

Jessica sighed. "Listen, Elizabeth. I don't know if this is a good time to play goody-goody. *Everyone's* sinking to their level."

"What do you mean, *everyone?*" Elizabeth asked.

Jessica took a step closer. "Well, I didn't want to upset you, but I saw the Gilberts putting sneezing powder in the Parkers' sweaters."

"What?" Elizabeth squealed.

"Of course, the Parkers happened to see that too—just in time," Jessica went on. "They didn't get near their sweaters, but they *did* manage to put a little ketchup in the Gilberts' blush." She giggled. "You noticed that their makeup looked a little funny, right?"

"Jessica!" Elizabeth exclaimed. "How can you laugh about something like that?"

"Look, all I'm saying is that we have to—"

"Be more careful," Elizabeth finished. She took the can of soda from Jessica, drained it, and threw it in the industrial-size garbage can. "Come on. And keep your eyes open."

"Kick . . . kick . . . turn left . . . kick kick . . . turn right . . . kick kick . . . skip . . . and skip . . . and . . ." Shirley was leading the group through the combination again.

Elizabeth moved lightly, feeling incredibly graceful. Suddenly Elizabeth had a funny feeling. She turned her head and realized that Jenny Pearman was dancing awfully close to her.

"Kick . . ."

Elizabeth felt something brush her ankle. *Jenny's foot!* She moved slightly to the left to avoid it.

"Elizabeth," Marian shouted over the music, "please don't break the line."

Elizabeth moved back into her original spot. She gave Jenny the dirtiest look she could. Jenny returned it with a bland smile.

Elizabeth turned her attention back to Shirley at the front. Moments later she felt something brush her ankle again. Elizabeth jumped to the side and out of ankle-kicking range.

"Elizabeth, please!" Marian shouted impatiently. "It's a precision drill. I thought you understood that!"

Elizabeth's cheeks flamed red with embarrassment. *I do! And if Jenny Pearman would quit trying to kick me, I might be able to dance it right!*

Jessica watched Elizabeth and Jenny in the mirror.

"Skip left . . . skip left . . . skip . . ."

Elizabeth jumped so far to the left, she bumped into Jessica.

"Elizabeth!" Marian barked. "What's the matter now?"

Jenny Pearman's psyched her out, Jessica thought. *That's what's the matter!*

She saw Jenny wink at Tricia in the mirror. Tricia smirked and smothered a giggle behind her hand.

Jessica gritted her teeth. Jenny Pearman had Elizabeth right where she wanted her now. All she had to do was *look* at Elizabeth and Elizabeth would reflexively move to avoid getting tripped or kicked.

It was the oldest trick in the world. Jessica had seen it a million times on the basketball court. Players could psych out their opponents and fool them into fouling themselves.

The pianist thrummed his thumb up and down the keyboard in a dramatic finale. *It's a good thing for you, Jenny, that Elizabeth is such a nice person,* Jessica thought angrily as she dropped down on one knee for the finish. *If it were me, I'd get you back if it was the last thing I did.*

During the break Elizabeth stood in the hallway, her lips and hands trembling. She couldn't go into the bathroom and cry. There were too many girls in there.

All she could do was stand there, take deep breaths, and try not to look as upset as she felt. She went over to the water fountain and bent her head to take a sip.

"Gosh, Elizabeth. You were doing so well. What happened?" someone asked in a saccharine voice.

Elizabeth lifted her head and saw Jenny Pearman beside her at the fountain. Jenny's green eyes were full of fake concern. The corners of her mouth quivered, as though she was trying not to smile.

Elizabeth's throat was too tight to answer. She took another drink and walked away without giving Jenny another glance.

She moved several feet down the hallway and leaned against the wall. Moments later Louise and Tammy came out of the rest room, got sodas out of the machine, and came over to join her.

"I heard Marian tell Jack that they're going to take some test film of us dancing after the break," Louise said.

Before Elizabeth could respond, Jenny bopped over beside them. "Did I hear you say they're going to shoot some test film?" Jenny asked eagerly.

Louise nodded. "That's right."

Jenny smiled. "Great. Tricia and I always look incredible on film. It's our eyes." Jenny fluttered her eyelashes dramatically, then let out a cry. "Oh, no!" She slapped a hand over her eye.

But she was a split second too late. Elizabeth had caught a glimpse of her eye. A *brown* eye!

Tinted contacts! The famous Pearman green eyes were fake!

"What's the matter?" Louise asked Jenny.

"My contact," Jenny said in a panicky voice. "I think I lost it." She leaned over and began frantically searching the floor.

Elizabeth's eyes flickered across the floor and spotted a small green disk less than an inch from Tammy's shoe. Her lips were just forming the words "There it is" when Tammy moved her foot so that her heel hovered over the contact lens.

Elizabeth's eyes flew upward and found Tammy staring right at her. Tammy's brow lifted, asking Elizabeth a silent question.

I should say something, Elizabeth thought. *I should tell Jenny that her contact is right there. It's the right thing to do. It's the nice thing to do.*

But then she remembered Jenny's foot on her ankle. The curt impatience of Marian's voice. The embarrassment of being chastised in front of everybody else. Most of all, she was angry that Jenny had spoiled her pleasure in the music and the movement.

Elizabeth felt her heart harden. She looked Tammy right in the eye and shut her mouth with a snap.

Tammy smiled. She lowered her heel to the floor and swiveled it back and forth slightly, silently grinding the green contact lens into the dusty floor—only inches away from where Jenny Pearman's hands frantically searched.

Five

◇

"Elizabeth, great! Jessica, great! You're looking good. You're looking great!" Marian walked up and down the front of the room. Jack followed with a camera.

Jessica broadened her smile as she kicked. The thrill of performing in front of a camera electrified her. Elizabeth seemed to have found her confidence again and was dancing like a pro.

But Jenny Pearman was apparently having a hard time.

"Hey! Ow!" Raquel Carver shouted. She doubled over and grabbed her thigh. "Jenny kicked me again!"

"Jenny!" Marian said impatiently. "That's the third time. Please keep your place in line."

Jessica smiled happily. What a stroke of good luck! Jenny Pearman had lost a contact. Not only couldn't she see to dance properly, she looked a little strange with one brown eye and one green eye. Jessica had noticed the double take Marian had done when she'd gotten a good look at Jenny after the break. Ha! The Pearman twins were history now.

Elizabeth dropped down on one knee, a huge smile on her face. They had danced the combination from start to finish. She'd been perfectly positioned and hadn't missed a single beat.

Marian, Jack, and Shirley gathered at the piano and conversed in whispers.

One by one the kids rose to their feet, exchanging nervous glances. There would be more cuts now. Who would it be?

Marian nodded and scribbled as Jack and Shirley whispered in her ear. After a few moments she nodded briskly, then turned toward the group. She referred to her notes. "Erica and Michaela Stein, Betty and LuAnn Lundgren, Katie and Kathy McMahon, Teresa and Cassandra Jackson, Jenny and Tricia Pearman, Raquel and Casey Carver . . ."

We're being eliminated. Despite all her reservations about sticking with the audition, Elizabeth felt her stomach sink with disappointment.

". . . Penny and Polly Gilbert, and Chrissy and Tiffany Peterson, I'm sorry, but you're not what we're looking for at this time. Thank you very much."

Elizabeth felt as though her heart might burst through her chest. Only two pairs had made the cut. Her and Jessica and . . . Tammy and Louise!

Elizabeth found herself eyeball to eyeball with Tammy Parker again.

"Congratulations," Tammy said with a smile— the same smile she had worn while grinding Jenny Pearman's contact into the floor.

Marian motioned Elizabeth, Jessica, Louise, and Tammy over to the piano. The four girls hurried to hear what she had to say. Marian opened her calendar and flipped the pages briskly. "Let me see . . . OK, I want all four of you back here to read for the part next Wednesday. We're waiting for scripts to be delivered from the production office. As soon as we receive them, we'll messenger them to you. Please study the lines that we highlight and be ready to do the scene from memory. And please prepare a song to sing." She smiled at the group. "You are four very talented girls. May the best pair win!"

"Ah-*choo!*" Steven's sneeze was loud and explosive.

"Do you *mind?*" Jessica said irritably. "Don't you realize that Elizabeth and I are poised on the brink of stardom? I can't afford to catch a cold right now."

Jessica, Steven, and Mr. and Mrs. Wakefield were gathered in the kitchen preparing dinner. Elizabeth was upstairs soaking her tired muscles in a hot bath.

"Hey!" Steven retorted. "This was *your* cold. You had it last week and you gave it to me."

"Well, I don't want it back," Jessica answered. She pulled a knife from the slotted wooden knife holder on the counter and began slicing a cucumber for the salad.

Mrs. Wakefield gathered knives and forks from a drawer. "Jessica's right. Steven, you're probably a health hazard. Go up to bed. And that's an order. You've been sneezing and sniffling for two days now. I'm making it official. You have a cold."

"Mom!" Steven protested.

"You heard your mother," Mr. Wakefield said sternly, stirring the spaghetti sauce. "You're sick and you're not going to get any better unless you go to bed and stay there."

"I'll bring you up some soup and some tea," Mrs. Wakefield said.

"And I'll be up to paint *quarantined* across your door," Jessica told him. She finished slicing the cucumber and placed two slices over her eyes.

"Gross!" Steven commented on his way out of the kitchen. "Don't bring me any salad," he told his mother. "You don't know where it's been."

"Jessica!" Mrs. Wakefield laughed. "What are you doing?"

"I read in a movie magazine that Connie Boyer puts cucumber slices on her eyes every morning and every night to keep from getting bags," Jessica explained.

Mr. Wakefield chuckled. "If you say so. Now would you mind grating the carrots? And we don't have a lot of carrots, so please don't use them for a beauty pack."

"Ha ha," Jessica said. "You're laughing now, but pretty soon Elizabeth and I are going to be stars. Big *big* stars."

She put her cucumbers back over her eyes. They felt cool, and they had a nice sweet smell. . . .

"Are the cucumbers cool enough?" Lila asked in a worried voice.

Jessica lay on her purple silk bedroom chaise with cucumbers over her eyes, a grated-carrot beauty mask over her face, and her hair slathered with olive oil. "Too cold," Jessica answered irritably. "How many times do I have to tell you, Lila? I like my cucumber slices at room temperature." She removed them from her eyes and frowned at her cringing assistant.

"I'm sorry." Lila reached for the nail file. "I'll try to remember." She lifted Jessica's limp hand and buffed her inch-long fingernails.

Jessica looked around the bedroom of her Beverly Hills mansion. It had everything she had ever wanted: one wall covered with life-size posters of Johnny Buck, another wall covered with CDs, and an enormous television screen for the third wall. A huge carousel unicorn stood in the corner.

Lila followed Jessica's gaze. "That unicorn is so cool," Lila said.

"It was a Christmas present from Johnny Buck," Jessica told her. "I told him about our old club, and he sent it to me as sort of a sentimental thing."

"The Unicorn days seem like a lifetime ago," Lila said with a sad sigh.

Jessica got up, went into the bathroom, and stepped into her six-jet shower. She turned on the hot water and lathered up with the herbal shampoo and body soap that had been created especially for her.

She rinsed off, got out of the shower, wrapped her hair in a purple turban, and donned a bathrobe covered with purple sequins.

"It does seem like a lifetime ago," Jessica said, sweeping back into the bedroom with the train of her robe trailing behind. "But so much has changed. I'm as rich as you are now. But I'm a famous movie star and you're not."

"When are you going to introduce me to some of your famous friends?" Lila asked.

"You're just not cool enough yet, Lila," Jessica responded.

"But I'm working as your assistant so I can learn how to be cool," Lila protested. "I'm doing my best."

"Yes," Jessica said. "But your best just isn't good enough." She picked up one of the cucumber slices and examined it sadly. "Lila, if I can't trust you to get my cucumber slices the right temperature, how can I trust you not to embarrass me in front of my movie-star friends?"

After dinner Elizabeth was too keyed up to do homework. Her mind was full of music and dance steps . . . and smashed green contacts.

The incident weighed on her conscience.

Keeping silent while Tammy crushed Jenny's lens hadn't been a nice thing to do. But Jenny Pearman wasn't a nice person, she reminded herself sternly. What goes around comes around. Live by the sword, die by the sword.

"They're tough," Jessica had said.

Now Elizabeth was learning to be tough. And

that was good. Elizabeth liked tough women. She admired them.

She threw herself on the living room sofa, picked up the remote, and flipped to the classic movie channel. One of her very favorite movies was on. *The Big Story* was an old black-and-white movie about a woman reporter who outwits her fellow reporters and gets the big story. *She's tough,* Elizabeth thought. *And she doesn't feel guilty about being tough. So why should I?*

She listened to the fast dialogue, the witty repartee, the straightforward manner of the leading actress. *I'd like the chance to play a part like that,* Elizabeth thought.

Elizabeth hurried out of the Sixers office wearing a fedora and a jacket with big shoulder pads.

"Where are you going, sister?" a voice asked.

Elizabeth turned around. "Todd!" Elizabeth's special friend, Todd, stood beside the lockers wearing a 1930s-style suit. "Why are you wearing that suit?" she asked. "And why are you calling me sister?"

"For the same reason you're wearing that fedora and jacket," Todd explained. "It's the 1930s and we're hard-boiled newspaper reporters. You can call me pal. Or buster."

"OK, pal," Elizabeth said, pulling her fedora down over her left eye. "What brings you to Sweet Valley Middle School?"

"I'm looking for a big story. I got an anonymous phone tip that said a sixth-grader got a big part in a new movie."

"Oh, yeah?" Elizabeth lifted one eyebrow, looking

very cynical. "Don't believe everything you hear."

"You mean it's not true?" Todd asked.

Elizabeth laughed. "I can't believe you actually fell for that old joke. Ten to one that so-called tip was from Jessica Wakefield. You know she's crazy to get into show biz, and she's always trying to get her name in the paper."

Todd closed his notebook and put it into the inside pocket of his jacket. "Darn! If it had been true, and I'd gotten an exclusive interview, I'd have been a real hero to my editor."

"Better luck next time." Elizabeth followed Todd out of the building and watched him climb onto his bicycle. As soon as he had ridden out of sight, Elizabeth ran back into the building and down the hall to the cafeteria.

Just as she thought. The big story was sitting right there at the Unicorner. Elizabeth smiled and swaggered over to where the next big star of stage and screen was eating lunch with her Unicorn friends. With Todd out of the way, the story was all hers. She whipped out her reporter's notebook. "Miss Wakefield!" she said.

Jessica Wakefield wiped a streak of mustard from her cheek and peered at Elizabeth over the tops of her rhinestone-studded sunglasses. "Yes?"

"I'm with the Sixers," Elizabeth said. "Is it true you're starring in the biggest movie of the season? We've heard it before, you know."

Jessica Wakefield smiled. "Yes, but this time it's really true. And since you're the first reporter to believe me, I'm going to give you an exclusive interview."

Elizabeth chuckled and sat down. Poor Todd. He'd

probably get fired for missing the big story. But that's what he got for being a sucker. You had to look out for yourself in the newspaper business. And it paid to be tough.

In the kitchen, Jessica plunged her hand into the box of Corny O's and shoved a bunch into her mouth. Whenever she got nervous, she liked to munch. And she'd been getting more and more nervous all night.

Jessica didn't trust Louise and Tammy Parker. If they could sandbag Jessica and Elizabeth somehow, they would.

Jessica's stomach tightened at the thought. They'd probably try some kind of dirty trick. But what? She tapped her finger against the edge of the Corny O's box and wandered through the dining room and into the living room.

She stood behind the sofa, staring at the TV over Elizabeth's head, her mind on Tammy and Louise Parker. She rattled the box, letting the cereal settle.

"Would you please stop that?" Elizabeth asked irritably.

"What's the matter with you?" Jessica asked. "Why are you so grouchy?"

Elizabeth clicked off the TV and turned. "I've been thinking about this audition thing. Do you think Louise and Tammy might try to sabotage us?"

"Yep!" Jessica said. "And it's making me nervous just sitting around waiting for them to make their move."

"What do you suggest?" Elizabeth asked.

Jessica climbed over the back of the sofa and offered the box to Elizabeth. "I've got an idea. But it's not pretty," she warned. "You probably won't want to go along with it."

Elizabeth reached in and grabbed a handful of cereal, then munched intensely. "Try me."

Six

"Mom and Dad are going to be really upset when they find out you're *both* insane," Steven said thickly. He settled his covers around him and reached for a tissue. "Now please go away and let me sleep. I feel awful." He stretched out his legs, trying to shove Jessica off the foot of his bed.

Jessica settled herself firmly on his legs, holding him prisoner. "No. We're not going away until you say you'll help us."

Steven reached for his glass of orange juice. Elizabeth grabbed it and held it just out of reach. "Well?" she asked.

"This is blackmail!" Steven's hoarse voice broke. "And besides, it's the stupidest idea I ever heard. I've never even seen these girls before. How am I supposed to get close enough to sneeze on them?"

Jessica smiled. "We looked up their address in the phone book. They don't live far away at all. You just go ring the bell. Chances are Louise or Tammy will answer the door, because they're waiting for their scripts, just like we are. When they open the door, say you're a newspaper carrier and ask them if they want to subscribe. Give them this flyer and then sneeze."

Elizabeth handed him some fake flyers she had printed on her computer. They said "Support Your Local Newspaper Carrier!" "Here. Breathe all over these and then hand one to each of them. Ninety percent of cold germs are transmitted via the hands."

Jessica grinned. "We figure if it took a strong, healthy basketball player less than a week to catch our cold, Louise and Tammy ought to have it in a couple of days. Then they'll be too sick to audition."

Steven blew his nose and gave Elizabeth a sorrowful look. "This is exactly the kind of loony plan I'd expect from Jessica. But I'm really disappointed in you, Elizabeth." He held out his hand. "Now hand over that orange juice."

Elizabeth drew it another few inches away.

Jessica reached into the back pocket of her jeans and removed an advertisement she had ripped from a magazine. She thrust the glossy and seductive page into Steven's hands.

"What's this?" he asked.

"It's a picture of an XT-540," Jessica said. "The most expensive high-performance car on the market.

Elizabeth and I figure that if we get the part, we ought to be able to afford it, easy."

"Wow!" Steven said.

"Movie stars make a lot of money," Elizabeth confirmed. "When we hit it big, we're going to need a manager. And that manager's going to need a fancy car to drive us around in. We're just trying to find out if you're management material."

Steven gave a mighty heave with his legs and knocked Jessica off the bed. He threw back the covers and rolled out of bed, planting his feet on the floor with a thump. "Call me Typhoid Murray and hand me my jeans."

Elizabeth hovered at the open door of her mother's office. Her mother was leaning over the desk, working on a sketch for a hotel lobby.

"Mom?" Elizabeth said softly.

"Mmm?" Mrs. Wakefield answered absently.

"Can I talk to you?" Elizabeth asked.

Mrs. Wakefield reached for a green pencil and began shading in the drapery on her drawing. "Mmm-hmmm."

Elizabeth looked up the stairs. Steven was moving slowly to the bottom, tiptoeing as quietly as he could.

"It's kind of private," Elizabeth said. "Mind if I close the door?" Without waiting for an answer, Elizabeth shut the door.

Mrs. Wakefield removed the blue pencil from her mouth. "Is something wrong?"

Suddenly Elizabeth's mind went blank. It had seemed so simple in the planning stage: Distract her mother while Steven sneaked out of the house. Now she had her mother's attention, but how was she supposed to keep her distracted?

"Elizabeth?" Mrs. Wakefield prompted. "Are you sick?"

"No!" Elizabeth cried. She didn't want her mom confining *her* to her room. "I was just wondering . . . um . . . well . . . if Jessica and I *do* get the part, will it be OK for us to miss school?"

Mrs. Wakefield laughed. "That's a big if. But if you do, then I suppose the movie company will make arrangements for you to keep up with your studies on the set and . . ." Mrs. Wakefield broke off and walked over to the window. "That looks like . . . it *is*!" Mrs. Wakefield raised the window. "Steven Wakefield!" she shouted. "You come back in this house right now!"

"Get in that bed and don't you even *think* of leaving this house," Mrs. Wakefield scolded. "You've got a temperature and a cough, and I don't want this turning into pneumonia. Do you understand?"

"Yes, Mom," Steven croaked. "I'm sorry. I just thought I'd run over to the video place and save you a trip. I know you're busy."

"Call your dad at the office," Mrs. Wakefield said. "He went for an hour or so to look over some papers. I'm sure he'll be happy to stop and rent you a video on his way home. Now get back into your pajamas and please try to rest."

Jessica and Elizabeth hid behind the door of Elizabeth's room, peeking through the crack at Mrs. Wakefield, who stood in Steven's doorway.

"What are we going to do now?" Elizabeth whispered.

"If at first you don't succeed, try, try again," Jessica whispered back.

Mrs. Wakefield turned and descended the steps.

Jessica and Elizabeth darted across the hall and into Steven's room. He was in his pajamas and was climbing back into bed.

"Stop!" Jessica cried.

Steven paused. "Now what?"

Jessica closed his door and hurried to the window. She raised it, looked outside, and then motioned him over. "Come on. The coast is clear."

"You want me to climb out the window?" Steven squeaked.

Jessica tapped her foot. "You have a better idea?"

"Yeah," Steven said with a laugh. "I get back in bed and you two go do whatever it is you do on a Saturday. Gossip with your friends or whatever."

"I resent that!" Elizabeth said hotly. "I do *not* gossip, and for your information—"

"Hey!" Jessica said sharply. Sometimes it was hard to keep Elizabeth's mind on track. "Let's not get off the subject here." She turned to Steven and smiled. "Aren't you forgetting that XT-540?"

"What good is it going to do me if I'm grounded?" Steven demanded. "Or *dead!*" he added.

Jessica waved her hand in a dismissive fashion. "When we're raking in the big bucks, Mom and Dad will forget all about this little incident. Trust me."

Steven coughed. "When you're raking in the big bucks, you give me a call. Until then, you'll have to manage yourselves."

Jessica snatched his jeans off the floor and waved them. "OK. Look. We'll sweeten the deal. We'll throw in a ski condo."

Steven grinned. "A ski condo?" he repeated in a pleased voice.

"With a snowmobile," Elizabeth added.

Steven's eyes glinted.

"But of course nobody wants to ski all the time," Jessica said. "So you'd need a beach house too. And a surfboard."

Steven groaned. "OK, OK, you got me." He took the jeans from Jessica and pulled them on over his pajama bottoms. He glanced at Elizabeth. "You realize that neither one of us ever had a chance, don't you?"

Elizabeth nodded sadly. "I know. But that's just the way it is." She gave his hand a pat.

Steven shrugged on a jacket and walked to the window with a dragging, martyrlike gait. "It's a far, far better thing I do here," he intoned in a dramatic voice, "than I have ever done before."

Jessica opened the window and practically shoved him out of it. "Whatever. Just get going. The sooner you start sneezing, the sooner those germs can start spreading."

"Bye, Mom," Elizabeth shouted. "We're going to pick up a video for Steven."

"That's nice," Mrs. Wakefield answered from inside the office.

Elizabeth and Jessica ran outside and closed the door behind them. They had given Steven a ten-minute head start to shimmy down the rose trellis and get safely out of sight before they left.

Elizabeth broke into a run. "Come on," she said. "I want to get there in time to watch."

Jessica panted loudly. Keeping up with Steven was work—even when he was sick, he moved fast. She and Elizabeth had practically jogged from their house, and Steven had been several yards ahead of them the whole distance.

"Shhh!" Elizabeth warned.

Jessica put her hand over her mouth, trying to keep her breathing quiet. They bent down to hide behind the four-foot-high boxwood hedge that bordered the Parkers' yard.

Steven glanced nervously over in their direction.

Jessica waved her hand, telling him to go on up to the door.

Steven patted his hair, lifted his flyers and

coughed all over them, then squared his shoulders. He was just about to start up the walk when the front door swung open.

Steven dove sideways so that he was hidden behind the hedge on the other side of the walkway.

"Bye, Mom!" one of the twins yelled. "We're going to the Chad's Burgers. Be back in an hour."

Jessica and Elizabeth peered through the thick leaves of the hedge. Louise and Tammy were coming down the walk. Jessica grabbed Elizabeth's arm and they backed up, rounding the corner of the hedge just as Louise and Tammy reached the sidewalk.

Now Jessica and Elizabeth were hiding on the side of the hedge *inside* the yard. Jessica looked over at Steven. He shot her a questioning look.

Jessica jabbed her finger in the direction of the departing Parker twins. "Follow them!" she mouthed.

Steven sneaked back around the hedge, crossed the street, and began following Louise and Tammy at a discreet distance. Jessica and Elizabeth gave them a few minutes' head start, then crossed the street and trailed behind.

"They're going in," Elizabeth whispered. "They're sitting down at a table . . . they're looking at menus."

"I'm right here," Jessica said irritably. "You don't have to give me a play-by-play."

"Sorry," Elizabeth muttered. "I got carried away." She and Jessica peered in the window of the Chad's Burgers.

Steven was sitting down at a table on the other side of the restaurant.

"Why is he sitting *there?*" Jessica whispered furiously. She waved her hand.

Steven did a slight double take when he spotted the twins in the window.

Jessica jabbed her finger in the direction of the Parker twins. "Sit closer!" she hissed.

Elizabeth's stomach tightened. They were counting on Steven to come through for them. She hoped he wasn't chickening out. It was a dirty job, but somebody had to do it. Elizabeth jabbed her own finger, egging him on. "I feel like Lady Macbeth," she whispered.

"Lady who?" Jessica asked.

"Somebody who probably started out as a good kid, the way I did." Elizabeth shook her head. "I can't believe I'm actually conspiring to give two people a cold. This isn't like me."

"Just goes to show you never know what you can do until you try," Jessica agreed cheerfully.

Steven had never felt so conspicuous in his life. He felt sure that everybody was wondering what that guy with the big red nose was doing sitting in the Chad's Burgers by himself—with the legs of his pajamas hanging out of his jeans.

As discreetly as possible, Steven stuffed the striped hems into his socks so that they wouldn't show. He squinted at the list of daily specials, which was written in colored chalk on a board near the counter. He craned his neck, as if he couldn't read the board from where he sat. Then he got up and moved closer, pretending to be reading. He slowly lowered himself into a chair at a table next to the Parker girls.

He felt a big sneeze coming on. He leaned as close as he could to them. "Ahhhh . . . ahhhh . . . ahhhh-choooo!"

Even Steven was impressed. He'd had no idea he had that much firepower. He could just imagine the germs bouncing off the back wall.

Louise and Tammy recoiled. Steven pulled a napkin from the chrome holder and wiped his nose. "Excuse me," he said. "I don't have my glasses. Could you please tell me what the hamburger special is today?"

One of the girls sighed, as though she couldn't believe he was bugging them. "I'm sure the waiter will be happy to tell you," she said impatiently. She turned back to her sister and began to talk in a low tone.

Steven sat there for a moment, frowning. They'd really given him the brush-off. Who did they think they were anyway? As far as he was concerned, they should be *flattered* that he was trying to talk to them. After all, he was a pretty good-looking guy.

His nose began to tingle. "Excuse me," he said, leaning as close as he could. "Do you know what tiiii . . . tiiii . . . *ahhhh-choooo!* . . . time it is?"

The Parker twins both leaned back, looking disgusted. "I'm not wearing my watch," one of them said. She hid her hand under the table as she spoke. But Steven knew she was lying. He had seen the watch on her wrist. What a snot.

And speaking of . . . Steven blew his nose in a napkin and then wadded it up, dropping it on the tabletop just to gross them out. He leaned as close as he dared, until he was inches from one of the twins. "Can I ask you a personal question?" he wheezed.

"What?" the girl asked from between gritted teeth.

"Are you two identical twins?"

The other girl took her napkin and held it over her mouth and nose. "Come on, Louise," she said in a muffled voice. "I think we'd be more comfortable sitting over there."

The two girls got up and moved several tables away. *Tap! Tap! Tap! Tap!*

Steven turned toward the window nearest him. He could see Jessica gesturing toward the Parker twins. Apparently she wanted him to follow them to their new table.

Steven shook his head. No. He'd given it his best shot. He wasn't about to come up with another lame excuse to go sneeze on them. He turned away. *Tap! Tap! Tap! Tap!*

He turned irritably. Jessica had the picture of the XT-540 plastered up against the glass. Then, just as suddenly as it had appeared, the picture disappeared.

Jessica and Elizabeth looked determined. This time both girls jabbed their fingers toward the Parkers.

Then, suddenly, their eyes widened and they ducked down out of sight.

Steven turned and realized the Parker girls were jabbing *their* fingers. At *him!* They seemed to be trying to point him out to a large, frowning man wearing an apron.

Uh-oh, Steven thought. *If this is who I think it is . . .*

"And *stay* out!" Clutching the back of Steven's jacket, the man pushed him out the door.

Steven hurtled past Jessica and Elizabeth and fell against some garbage cans by the curb. A crate of garbage balanced on top of a can teetered for a second or two, then toppled over, spilling its contents over his sprawled body.

The big man stood in the doorway and dusted off his hands. "I don't like young men who bother young ladies. I don't like young men who bother anybody!"

He closed the door with a slam.

Elizabeth and Jessica ran over to excavate Steven.

Jessica wrinkled her nose. "Pee-yew. Hard to believe this is the same stuff that smells so good coming out of the oven."

Elizabeth gingerly removed a layer of banana peels, crumpled napkins, pizza crusts, and cold, greasy french fries from her brother's head. "I never thought something like this would happen. I'm really, really sorry. We'll get you home and back to bed. Forget about helping us."

"What?" Steven protested weakly. "And give up show business?"

Seven

"Think it worked?" Jessica asked as she channel-surfed.

Elizabeth resisted the temptation to grab the remote from her sister's hand. She wished Jessica would find a channel and stick with it. All that switching around made her nervous. And she was nervous enough after the afternoon's events. "Probably not. Steven's a good sneezer, but I think you have to have closer contact to give somebody a cold. If he could have touched something that they touched, or sneezed on something they ate, that probably would have been more effective."

The twins had managed to sneak Steven back into the house without being seen, and he had just run upstairs to take a shower.

"Did you get anything good at the video place?"

The girls turned to see Mrs. Wakefield standing in the large arched doorway that separated the front hall from the living room.

Elizabeth was about to make up an answer when a curious look crossed Mrs. Wakefield's face. "Do you girls smell *garbage?*" she asked, sniffing the air.

"No." Jessica widened her eyes innocently. "Do you smell garbage, Elizabeth?"

Elizabeth swallowed. "Sorry, Mom. Don't smell a thing."

"Odd," Mrs. Wakefield commented absently, walking through the living room toward the kitchen.

Jessica jumped up. "I'm going upstairs to zap Steven's room with some air freshener. We don't want her sniffing out the truth!"

Jessica ran out of the room, and Elizabeth took the remote. She had just flipped to the classic movie channel when the doorbell rang.

She hopped off the couch to answer it, hoping it was Amy or Maria. She opened the door.

Nobody.

She stepped outside and looked up and down the street. She didn't see a soul. Elizabeth was just about to step back inside when she spotted the gift basket beside the door. She eagerly bent over to examine it.

It was a gorgeous basket filled with chocolates, fancy teas, and two big bottles of expensive-looking shampoo and conditioner. A little envelope was attached to the handle of the basket with a narrow gold ribbon. "To Elizabeth and Jessica," the envelope said.

Elizabeth eagerly opened it and removed a handwritten note.

> Dear Elizabeth and Jessica:
>   This is just our way of saying thanks for your hard work.
>   Sincerely,
>   Star Quality Casting
>
> P.S.: Your hair looked a little dull in the test film. We're enclosing a specially formulated hair product that will bring out your natural highlights. Please use it Wednesday morning.

Elizabeth closed the door and ran upstairs with the basket. "Jessica! Look what we got!"

Jessica stood in the upstairs hallway, holding her nose and spraying air freshener in every direction. "Sheesh! Steven really stank the place up. We may have to sneak his clothes out of the house and burn them. What's that?"

Elizabeth handed her the note and dug eagerly through the basket. "Look! Little chocolate stars! Isn't that neat?"

"Dull!" Jessica cried out in a panicky voice as she read the note. "Our hair looked *dull?*"

Elizabeth unwrapped a chocolate and popped it in her mouth. "Don't take it so personally. We'll use that shampoo on Wednesday and—"

Jessica grabbed the shampoo and conditioner

from the basket. "I'm not waiting until Wednesday. I'm using this right now."

Jessica ran off with the bottles. Elizabeth took the basket into her room and sat down on the bed. She sorted through the selection, impressed. Star Quality Casting had really gone all out.

Inside the bathroom that connected her room to Jessica's, she heard the shower go on. A couple of minutes later she heard a scream. "Elizabeth! Elizabeth! Come quick! Help!"

Elizabeth ran into the bathroom and peered around the shower curtain. "Oh, no!" she gasped.

"It's not coming off!" Jessica wailed.

Black goo, thick as tar, dribbled from Jessica's hair all down her body.

"You've been slimed," Elizabeth groaned.

"I must say, this was just about the worst hair day I've ever seen. But now you're as good as new." Grace, the hairdresser at Cut and Curl, drew her comb through Jessica's freshly washed and conditioned hair. It gleamed beneath the salon's fluorescent lights.

Jessica's eyes were as red as a rabbit's from all the chemicals. Three hairdressers had labored for two hours to get the tar and black dye out of her hair.

But the hardest part had been getting it off her face and forearms. All the fine hairs had taken the black dye. It had taken bleach, wax, and even a little pumice stone to remove it all.

Grace held out a hand mirror so that Jessica

could see her hair from all angles. "A little pink, maybe, from all the rubbing, but at least you don't look like you need a shave."

"Thank you," Jessica told the group gratefully. "We really appreciate it. Both of us. Right, Elizabeth?"

Elizabeth stood behind Jessica's chair and nodded. "I don't know what we would have done if you couldn't get it out."

Grace shook her head. "I've seen some nasty practical jokes in my time, but this was about the nastiest. Any idea who did it?"

"I know who did it," Jessica answered. "And believe me, from now on, it's *war!*"

"One phony script coming right up." Elizabeth took her yellow marker and highlighted a few sentences from the pages she'd just printed out. "I wrote this scene in that scriptwriting course I took last summer," she told Jessica. The highlighter squeaked as she marked the lines that called for bloodcurdling screams. "It's about two girls who run into a monster while exploring a cave. There, that's done. Now we need a cover letter."

Elizabeth turned back to her computer and began typing while Jessica leaned over her shoulder, reading from the monitor.

Dear Louise and Tammy,

As promised, here's the scene you will be reading for us on Wednesday. We are very

concerned that your screams sound as au-
thentic as possible, so we urge you to practice, practice, practice!

Sincerely yours,
Star Quality Casting

Jessica laughed. "If they spend the next two days
screaming their heads off, their voices will be shot
by Wednesday. They'll sound like sandpaper."

Elizabeth printed out the letter and reached for a
manila envelope. "Look out, Tammy and Louise,"
she said with a glimmer of satisfaction.

Twenty minutes later Jessica came running in the
front door. She had just sped home on her bike from
the Parkers', where she'd shoved the envelope in
their mail slot. Now she could hear the phone ring-
ing. And she just knew it was Tammy and Louise.

She ran into the kitchen and grabbed the phone just
as Elizabeth came hurrying in from the patio. "Hello?"
Jessica said, trying not to sound too breathless.

"May I speak to Jessica or Elizabeth?"

Jessica covered the mouthpiece of the phone. "It's
them," she hissed. "Should I say anything about the
shampoo?"

Elizabeth shook her head. "No. They don't
know we used it yet. Play dumb." She put her ear
to the phone so she could listen in.

"This is Jessica," Jessica said into the phone.

"Hello, Jessica. This is Louise Parker."

Louise's voice sounded really relaxed and pleasant, Jessica observed. As though everything was just fine and she didn't have a care in the world.

"What's up, Louise?" Jessica asked.

"We just received our copy of the script," Louise said, "and we wondered if you had received your copy."

Elizabeth nodded.

"Yes," Jessica said. "As a matter of fact, we have. And we've already started practicing." She gestured frantically to Elizabeth. Elizabeth opened her mouth and screamed bloody murder. Jessica covered her other ear with her hand so she could hear Louise through the phone. "We're practicing like crazy."

"Well," Louise said in a friendly voice, "we were just calling to wish you luck. We'll see you Wednesday."

Jessica gestured to Elizabeth again. Elizabeth let loose a scream that sounded as though she were being boiled in oil.

"See you Wednesday," Jessica shouted.

She replaced the receiver just as Mr. Wakefield came racing in from the living room. "What's going on?" he asked, looking around in every direction as if he expected to see an ax murderer.

Jessica giggled. "Nothing, Dad. We're just practicing our lines."

Mr. Wakefield's shoulders slumped with relief, and he rolled his eyes upward.

Elizabeth giggled. "Sorry, Dad."

The doorbell rang.

"I'll get it," Mrs. Wakefield called from down the hall. A few moments later she came into the kitchen with two manila envelopes. "One for each of you. From Star Quality Casting. I imagine it's your scripts."

"I thought you were practicing from their scripts," Mr. Wakefield said in bewilderment.

"Uh . . . that was *another* script." A cold sweat formed along Jessica's hairline, and her stomach felt suddenly sour.

"Well, could you please keep the screaming to a minimum?" he asked. "We do have neighbors, and we don't want them getting up a petition asking us to move."

He and Mrs. Wakefield disappeared into the living room.

Jessica opened her envelope and slid out a script in a Star Quality Casting binder. She looked at Elizabeth. "Oops!"

"There goes our plan," Elizabeth said. "If we got these scripts, then so did Louise and Tammy. And that means they'll know that the script we sent them is a phony."

Jessica went over to the window and looked outside. Then she drew the curtains.

"What are you doing?" Elizabeth asked.

"It's only a matter of time before they strike back. We've got to be on our guard. Stay away from the doors and windows. Don't open the door for anyone, unless you know it's me. And don't eat or drink anything you didn't prepare yourself."

She turned out the lights. "I saw this in a movie once. The police were trying to hide a witness that the mob wanted to rub out."

"Wow." Elizabeth smiled wryly. "I'll never say watching TV is a waste of time again."

"But Ramona, if we run away tonight, we'll miss the recital," Elizabeth said. "Can't we go tomorrow?"

"We have to leave tonight! There's no plane tomorrow," Jessica replied.

"That's *train*," Elizabeth corrected her.

Jessica looked back down at the page. "Oh, yeah. Train. Sorry." She lowered her script. "We have to leave tomorrow. There's no train tonight."

"We have to leave *tonight*," Elizabeth corrected. "There's no train *tomorrow!*"

Jessica flopped back on her pillows and groaned. "I'm so tired I can hardly talk."

Elizabeth closed her script. "It's late," she said. "Let's go to bed and get back to work on this tomorrow morning. It's been a pretty long day."

Jessica's head rolled sideways as she pretended she had fallen immediately into a deep sleep.

Elizabeth tried to take the script from her hands, but Jessica tightened her grip and tugged. "Leave it," she said sleepily. "Maybe I can learn the lines by osmosis."

Elizabeth laughed. "OK. And if it works, let's try it with our history homework." She snapped off the light by Jessica's bed. "I'll see you in the morning."

Elizabeth went through the bathroom connecting her room and Jessica's and climbed into her own bed. As soon as she lay down she realized exactly how tired she was. Her legs felt like dead weights, and her arms and shoulders ached as the tense muscles began to relax.

She turned, settled her head more comfortably on her pillow and let herself drift into sleep. . . .

Elizabeth and Jessica sat in a train, hurtling through Sweet Valley. When they passed Sweet Valley Middle School, Elizabeth leaned out the window and waved at Amy and Todd and Maria. "Good-bye," she called out. "I'll call you when we get to Hollywood."

The train kept going, and Elizabeth saw Sweet Valley High. Steven stood on the front steps of the school in his pajamas. Elizabeth waved. He waved back.

"We're going to have to talk to Steven about his wardrobe if he's going to be our manager," Jessica said. "He'll look like an idiot driving around Los Angeles in his pajamas." The train made a screeching sound. "Hey! We're in Hollywood." Jessica's eyes brightened.

"But we can't be," Elizabeth argued. "We just left Sweet Valley."

"Then why is the train blowing its whistle?" Jessica asked. The screeching sound grew louder. "That's not the whistle." Elizabeth went pale. "Those are the emergency brakes."

Mr. Wakefield came running into the car, his face covered with shaving cream. "Emergency!" he shouted. "We've got an emergency!" Mrs. Wakefield came running in behind him. Black goo covered her blond hair.

Elizabeth jumped up. "Oh, no!" she shouted. "They got Mom by mistake!"

"Elizabeth!"

"They got Mom!" Elizabeth yelled.

"Elizabeth! Wake up!"

Elizabeth opened her eyes and blinked. Her bedside light was on, and Steven stood beside her. "You were having a nightmare," he said. "And no wonder. Listen to that!"

There was a horrible noise outside—a catfight, the loudest catfight Elizabeth had ever heard.

Jessica came through the bathroom, rubbing her eyes. "It's been going on forever," she complained. "You'd think they'd get tired by now."

"Sounds like they're just getting warmed up," Steven said. "Well, I'm going back to bed. If I close my door, I won't hear a thing—unless Elizabeth starts yelling again." He ambled across the hall and shut his door with a loud thud.

"In the movies, people throw boots out the window when they hear cats."

"Don't even think about it," Elizabeth warned. "If you want to throw a boot out the window, throw one of yours." She turned off the light and pulled the covers up over her head.

The yowling continued.

It was no use. Nothing could blot out the horrible sound.

Eight

◇

"Wow!" Steven said the next day at breakfast. "You guys look terrible."

"You don't look so good yourself," Jessica retorted.

Elizabeth sat down at the breakfast table, too exhausted even to participate in the argument.

Actually, neither Jessica nor Steven looked very good. Steven's nose was red and swollen and his eyes were puffy. Jessica had bluish circles under her eyes.

"What time did the dueling cats wrap it up?" Steven asked, pouring his customary mountain of cereal into a bowl.

"I don't know," Jessica answered dully. "A long time. I don't think I ever got back to sleep."

"Me either," Elizabeth said, finally summoning the energy to talk. Jessica passed her the cereal box, and Elizabeth filled her bowl. She began spooning sugar onto her cereal.

"I thought you didn't believe in putting sugar on cereal," Steven said.

"I don't," Elizabeth replied. "But at this point I'll take any energy source I can find—even refined white sugar." She looked at Jessica. "But Ramona, if we run away tonight, we'll miss the recital. Can't we go tomorrow?"

"We have to leave tonight!" Jessica responded listlessly. "There's no plane tomorrow."

"No!" Elizabeth snapped. "Think about what you're saying, would you?"

"Don't bite my head off," Jessica snapped back.

"I can't help it," Elizabeth said. "This is just so typical. We've gone to all this trouble to get the audition, and now you're going to blow it because you won't learn the lines."

"Hey, wait a minute. Who says I'm going to blow it?" Jessica's voice rose angrily.

Elizabeth swallowed the lump in her throat. She knew she was being mean to Jessica, but she was too upset to care. And too exhausted. She pushed her bowl away. She was too weary to eat. Or talk.

"I'll get the lines right. I'm just tired right now," Jessica said in a grouchy voice. "And so are you. We'll work this afternoon and get a good night's sleep tonight, and by tomorrow we'll have it down perfectly."

*   *   *

"Ramona! Michelle's USO unit was captured by the enemy." Elizabeth glanced at the script notes, which called for her character to cry. "We'll never find her now." A sob rose in her voice, and tears streamed down her cheeks.

"Wow! Elizabeth, that's great. You look like you're really crying," Jessica said.

"I *am* really crying," Elizabeth wailed. "That noise is driving me insane."

It was almost midnight. The girls had tried to sleep, but the neighborhood cats were back on the rampage. It was impossible to go to sleep with all that noise, so they had decided they might as well go over their lines again.

There was a clap of thunder outside, and then rain began beating down against the window.

"Elizabeth, please!" Jessica said. "If you don't stop crying, I'll start to cry too. And if I cry, I'll get a headache and then I'll never get all these lines right." Her mouth trembled, and her eyes began to water.

The catfight continued unabated.

"I thought cats didn't like water." Elizabeth sniffled.

"I thought so too," Jessica said.

They sat in tired silence for a while, listening to the rain and the cats. Suddenly one cat's voice changed dramatically. Its high-pitched yowl became a low gargle.

"That is so weird!" Jessica shivered. "Those don't sound like any cats I ever heard. Think there's any such thing as mutant cats from outer space?"

The cat noises grew slower, deeper, and stranger.

Something clicked in Elizabeth's exhausted brain. "No," she said slowly, "I don't." She got up and pulled her yellow rain slicker off the hook in her closet. "I'm going out there to find out what's making that racket. And I'm going to tell it to *shut up!*"

"I'll bring the flashlight!" Jessica said.

A few moments later the girls slipped out the front door in rain slickers and rubber boots. They followed the sound of the cats. It was coming from behind the bushes under Elizabeth's window.

"Whatever it is, it's in there," Elizabeth whispered. "Shine the light and see what it is."

Jessica leaned into the shrubs and aimed the high-powered beam into the bushes.

Elizabeth peered over the leaves. "Is sleep deprivation making me see things?" she exclaimed.

"If it is, it's making me see the same thing." Jessica reached into the bushes, grabbed a handle, and yanked up a boom box blasting weird, distorted noises. "I don't believe this." She hit the stop button, and the noise stopped.

Jessica removed the cassette and stared at it. "It's a ninety-minute tape. I guess Louise and Tammy found a recording of a catfight, put it on continuous play, and then left it in the flower bed. They didn't count on rain ruining the tape player."

"Those Parker twins are just unbelievable," Elizabeth said as they stomped back up the front steps.

Jessica pulled off her wet boots and set them on the step beneath the overhang. "Who would *think* of that? Even *I* could never come up with something that diabolical."

Elizabeth just shrugged. She draped her dripping raincoat over the railing and went inside. Jessica did the same.

Back in the house, Jessica flopped on the sofa, and Elizabeth went into the kitchen to grab a box of Corny-O's. "So what are we going to do?" she asked, munching a handful of cereal as she returned to the living room. She sat down next to Jessica.

"We could try to sleep," Jessica answered, reaching for the Corny O's.

Elizabeth shook her head. "I'm way too wound up to sleep now." She picked up the remote control and turned on the TV. "Let's watch a movie and let our brains relax for a while."

Elizabeth surfed the channels.

"Hold it!" Jessica cried, jumping up and dropping the box of cereal. Corny O's spilled all over the floor. "It's her. I mean them."

"Who?" Elizabeth asked.

"Tammy and Louise. Go back. Go back."

Elizabeth began backtracking through the channels.

"There!" Jessica pointed at the TV screen. Sure enough, Louise Parker (or was it Tammy?) was right there in living color. "Boo!" Jessica sneered.

She clenched her fists. "Come out of there and fight like a woman."

"Shhh!" Elizabeth said. "I want to hear." She turned up the sound. Jessica came over and sat back down on the couch.

Elizabeth had to admit that Louise (or was it Tammy?) looked beautiful. Her eyes glowed, and her hair gleamed. The music swelled, and Louise began to sing.

"Think that's really her voice?" Jessica asked.

"I don't know," Elizabeth said nervously. "If it is, she's really good. I mean, she sounds like a professional." The Corny O's in her mouth suddenly tasted dry and flavorless. Louise sounded more than just professional. She sounded like a major talent.

"I'm sure it's dubbed," Jessica said. "She's lip-synching. When she starts to act, we'll see how amateurish she really is."

The song came to an end, and the character Louise was playing took a bow. The camera followed her as she ran backstage, where her mother and best friend, Willa, were waiting.

"Oh, Claire," her mother said, "you were wonderful."

Claire turned away from her mother as if she hadn't even heard. "Did you order my new ski clothes?" she asked in a petulant voice.

"No," her mother answered softly. "I haven't had time. I was working on your dress." Claire's mother shyly opened a closet and pulled out a beautiful beaded gown.

"She made it," Willa said. "She sewed on every bead by hand. She wanted you to have a special dress when you receive your Performer of the Year award."

Claire reached out and plucked a bead from the dress. She examined it in the palm of her hand. "Doesn't look like she did a very good job! It came right off."

Claire's mother let out a little cry, and Willa stared at her. "What kind of monster have you become?" she whispered. "I used to look up to you. I admired your talent, your drive. But you used me. And you used your mother. You used everybody. And now that you don't need us anymore, you treat us like dirt."

Claire's lip lifted in a snarl. "Then get out if you're so unhappy. Both of you. Get out of my life! And get out of my way!" Claire charged past Willa and her mother, practically knocking them over.

Elizabeth sat riveted as Claire yelled insulting remarks at all the stagehands and then went back onstage to do her encore. When she finished, the audience in the concert hall stood up and cheered. After the concert, Claire drove away in a Rolls-Royce.

Claire went to Paris and London and Rome. Everywhere she performed, audiences cheered. And Claire grew more and more arrogant.

Finally, in Berlin, Claire gave her most stunning performance. She expected a party to celebrate her success. But when she arrived at her hotel room, there was no one. No one had sent any flowers. No one had sent a note. No one had come by. There was no one to go to dinner with.

Claire went down to the hotel dining room and ate by herself. Across the dining room, she saw a group of girls laughing and talking. The camera closed in on a tear trickling down Claire's cheek. She was a famous star, but so what? She was miserable.

And she was all alone.

Elizabeth pulled a tissue from the box on the end table. "What a great movie!" she sobbed.

"Great?" Jessica aimed the remote at the TV. "I didn't think it was so great. Movies like that are all the same. They try to make you think it's lonely being rich and famous so that you won't feel bad if you aren't."

Elizabeth pulled the remote from Jessica's hands and wiped her tears. "Shhh! I want to see the credits." As they rolled by, Elizabeth squinted at the screen. "Claire was played by . . . Louise and Tammy Parker!"

Elizabeth shut off the TV and gave a last sniff. "We're toast. We might as well just call in on Wednesday and wish Louise and Tammy good luck in their movie career."

Jessica's eyes flashed. "Are you *kidding?*"

"Jessica, come on! They were good. They were *great.*" She studied Jessica's face closely. "Don't tell me you weren't moved. Your eyes look teary."

Jessica jerked her hand up to her face. Then she

let out a weary sigh. "OK, OK. I was moved. A little." She sniffed. "But we're just as good. Better."

"I'm sure we'll be *tons* better on no sleep for two nights in a row," Elizabeth said dryly.

Jessica's forehead creased in a frown. "We'll just have to get back at them somehow . . . make sure they don't sleep for a week . . . make them slip—"

"Jessica! Listen to yourself," Elizabeth broke in. "That movie's right—fame and fortune *do* turn people into monsters."

"This is just self-defense, Elizabeth," Jessica said firmly.

Elizabeth sighed. "I talked myself into believing that before. But just because the Pearmans and the Parkers were wrong doesn't mean the stuff we did was right. And I'm not about to turn into an even bigger monster by making anyone slip or—"

"All right already!" Jessica fell back against the pillows. "No more dirty tricks. But we can't just drop out of the audition."

Elizabeth sighed. "OK. We'll give it our best shot."

Jessica stared grimly at the television screen. "They *were* pretty good, weren't they?" she said in a small voice.

"Yeah. They were," Elizabeth agreed.

Jessica gave her the most pathetic look Elizabeth had ever seen. Elizabeth had the feeling that Jessica wouldn't dare say what they were both thinking: that next to talent like the Parkers', their best shot probably wouldn't be good enough.

Nine

◇

"Here we go," Elizabeth said, punching the button for the fourth floor. "Now remember, no matter what happens, we're going to be mature. Magnanimous. Bigger than they are."

"A fire hydrant is bigger than they are," Jessica said sourly.

Elizabeth laughed, determined to be cheerful. The elevator door slid open, and she stepped out into the hallway, smoothing her short brown corduroy skirt. She and Jessica didn't usually dress alike, but they'd improvised matching outfits that day. Jessica wore a short brown suede skirt. Both girls wore plain beige blouses, brown tights, and loafers. And they had both curled their hair and pulled it back on either side with matching barrettes.

The door to the rehearsal studio was open, and

Elizabeth could hear voices inside. She and Jessica entered. Louise and Tammy were already standing by the piano. They wore matching plaid dresses with puffed sleeves and wide patent leather belts.

"Those dresses are so babyish!" Jessica whispered.

"Shhh!" Elizabeth cautioned. But she had to admit to herself that the dresses *were* the kind of thing really little girls wore.

The Parker twins were going over some sheet music with the pianist while Jack and Marian whispered together over their copy of the script. They looked up and smiled at Elizabeth and Jessica. "Hi, girls!" Marian said. "I hope you're not nervous."

"We're not," Elizabeth answered. "We're looking forward to doing the scene."

Jack pumped his fist. "Yes! That's exactly the right attitude. It's important to have fun with the material."

Elizabeth turned to Tammy and Louise. "But before we start, Jessica and I have a couple of things we want to say."

"We do?" Jessica blinked in surprise.

"Last night this really awful catfight kept me and Jessica up late," Elizabeth began.

Tammy turned a little pale, and Louise bit her lip. Elizabeth smiled despite herself. She knew they were expecting her to accuse them of dirty tricks. But they were in for a surprise.

"So we decided to watch television, and just by chance we saw you guys in *Lights Out*. We just wanted to tell you how impressed we were with your performances. You did a great job. And even though we're going to give this audition our best shot . . . well, we know you guys really have what it takes. You've obviously paid your dues and learned your craft."

Elizabeth waited for Louise and Tammy to smile, say thanks, and shake hands all around. But neither one of them looked the least bit pleased. Louise looked as if she'd just been slapped. Her astonished mouth hung open slightly, and her eyes glowed angrily. Tammy's mouth formed a grim, malevolent line.

And Jack was frowning thoughtfully into the distance.

Elizabeth looked from face to face. What was wrong? What had she said? What had she done?

"*Lights Out*," Jack said slowly. "I had a friend who worked on that movie. That was a while ago, wasn't it?"

"Four years ago," the piano player put in, staring hard at Tammy and Louise.

Tammy's face immediately changed. Her eyes opened wide, and her mouth softened. "Oh, no!" she said in a childish, breathy voice. "It wasn't four years ago at *all*."

Louise launched into what seemed like a Shirley Temple imitation. She chuckled merrily. "Four years ago? No, no. We just finished that movie."

"It was four years ago," the piano player insisted in a steely tone. "I worked on the sound track for that film."

Marian began circling Tammy and Louise,

eyeing them closely from head to toe. "I'm beginning to realize why you two seemed so much more seasoned than the others," she said slowly. "You're a lot older than I thought, aren't you?"

The innocent looks disappeared from the twins' faces. They were little girls no longer. Their faces were older, harder, and really mean.

Suddenly Elizabeth understood the reason for the babyish dresses and the pigtails.

There was a long, tense, strained silence. Elizabeth realized she was holding her breath.

"All *right!*" Tammy practically spat. She snatched her music from the pianist's hands. "We *are* over the age limit. Sixteen, if you must know. So sue us." She grabbed her little patent leather purse off the top of the piano and turned to face Elizabeth and Jessica. "You act so sweet! So naive. Such nice little girls. 'You've obviously paid your dues and learned your craft,'" she piped in a high, sweet voice, mocking Elizabeth's speech.

Elizabeth felt her cheeks flaming red with anger. She had been prepared to be a good sport. Why couldn't they?

Tammy's angry eyes bored into Elizabeth's like lasers. "Pretending you weren't trying to sandbag us! Yeah, right. You *knew* what you were doing." She lifted her lip in a sneer. "You make me sick. Both of you. *Amateurs.* Come on, Louise."

Elizabeth watched Tammy and Louise stomp out of the studio, the hard soles of their Mary Jane shoes tapping noisily. They disappeared into the hall.

Elizabeth slowly let her breath out. Her heart was pounding. She realized her hands were shaking. She'd never seen anybody look so angry and hateful in her whole life.

Marian put one arm around Elizabeth's shoulders and the other arm around Jessica's. "Congratulations, girls. You've got the part."

Elizabeth knew she should be happy, but she was still dazed after Tammy's verbal attack. Things had taken such a sudden turn! She was still trying to take it all in.

But Jessica seemed to have no problem grasping the bottom line. *"We've got the part!"* she squealed happily. She threw her arms around Elizabeth. "We did it! We did it!" Then she released her twin so suddenly that Elizabeth stumbled backward.

"Who's in the movie?" Jessica asked eagerly. "I mean, besides us."

"Connie Boyer," Marian answered.

Jessica let out another delighted shriek. "Connie Boyer! She's my *idol!*"

Elizabeth was so stunned, she could hardly register everything Marian was telling her. But she caught the words "big roles for you two" and "rising twin stars."

Ten

◇

"Bring that camera in closer!" a man shouted across a huge soundstage. "Closer. Closer. Good." The man carefully picked his way through a maze of cables and equipment. He wore a jacket that said "Assistant Director." There seemed to be a lot of assistant directors. Jessica had been on the set only an hour and a half and she had already counted five.

She'd tried to count the number of stagehands and extras, but it was impossible. There seemed to be a thousand people. And everybody was amazingly busy. Jessica couldn't figure out how they all knew what to do.

A woman from wardrobe had told Jessica to have a seat and wait while she took Elizabeth off somewhere to be fitted and made up.

A man about her father's age wandered up and stood next to her, his hands on his hips. "This is my fifteenth movie and I still can't figure out what they're doing." The man wore a jacket that said "W. L. Productions." He was very tall, with sandy red hair and glasses.

"Are you an actor?" Jessica asked shyly.

The man laughed. "No. I'm Wallace Libby, the executive producer."

"Wow!" Jessica knew it was rude to stare, but she couldn't help it. She'd never seen a real executive producer before.

"Don't be so impressed," he teased. "Nobody else is."

Jessica wondered if Mr. Libby knew how little experience she and Elizabeth actually had. She didn't want him to have second thoughts about using two unknowns. Jessica lowered her eyelids and tried to look very knowledgeable. "Executive producers all say that," she said. "But everybody knows they're the real bosses."

"Theoretically," Mr. Libby replied with a laugh. "May I ask your name?"

"I'm Jessica Wakefield, and I'm . . ." Jessica couldn't help grinning. She'd waited her whole life to say it. "I'm an actress," she said nonchalantly.

Mr. Libby nodded, looking impressed. "Well, I'm very glad to know that my movie will feature such an attractive young performer."

"Wallace!" A mostly bald man whose few

remaining hairs were scraped back into a ponytail came hurrying over, a script under his arm. "We may need to make some changes in the shooting schedule."

Mr. Libby took the script and glanced over it. "OK. But if it changes the budget, we'll have to talk to the studio." Then he looked apologetically at Jessica, as if he'd forgotten something important. "Excuse my bad manners," he said. "Oliver, have you met Ms. Wakefield?"

Oliver smiled faintly. Jessica could tell he was too preoccupied to be really interested in meeting anybody.

"Jessica Wakefield, this is Oliver Mitchell, the director."

"*The* director?" Jessica asked. "Not an assistant director?"

"*The* director," Mr. Libby confirmed.

Jessica couldn't help feeling a little disappointed. She'd always thought of movie directors as being very handsome, but Oliver wasn't at all romantic-looking.

"You're one of our twins, right?" the director asked. Jessica nodded. "That's right."

"OK. Well, we may be doing part of the train scene today, so please be sure you know your lines, OK?" He turned back to Mr. Libby. "Let's go see Sam now. Because if I have to get a new budget approved . . ."

The two men walked off, Oliver Mitchell talking

quickly and waving his hands, Mr. Libby listening and nodding.

Jessica sat down and glanced at her thick script. Every time she looked at it, her heart gave a big thump. It *was* her dream come true. She could still hardly believe it.

After the audition, Marian had come over to their house and gone over their contract with Mr. Wakefield. The girls were going to be paid union scale for their work. They would be picked up at 5 A.M. every morning by a studio limousine and driven to the new Filmworld studio complex near Sweet Valley. They would be brought back home every evening. The filming was scheduled to be completed in a month. And Jessica and Elizabeth were in lots of major scenes.

Jessica searched the script for her own lines, which were highlighted.

"Get up," a voice ordered. "I want to sit down."

When Jessica looked up to see who was speaking to her so rudely, her eyes widened and her throat constricted.

Connie Boyer!

She was way taller than Jessica had imagined. She looked about six feet tall. Her hair was platinum blond and so perfectly coiffed it looked like a white helmet. Her mouth was outlined in dramatic red lipstick, and a long filter-tipped cigarette dangled from her lower lip.

"I said get up, kid."

Jessica hopped up immediately. "Yes, ma'am," she managed to say.

Connie Boyer threw herself into the chair and crossed her legs. She eased her foot out of a pump with a three-inch spiked heel and rubbed her big toe. She drew on the cigarette and expelled smoke through her nose. "What are you looking at?" she asked in a surly voice.

Jessica swallowed, realizing that she had been staring. "I'm sorry. I've just never seen a movie star up close before."

Connie grunted and lowered her eyelids, as if she was bored with Jessica's admiration.

"I'm Jessica Wakefield," Jessica said, summoning up all her courage to speak to her idol. "I'm an actress too."

Connie Boyer stared at her. "Yeah?" She removed the cigarette from her mouth and dropped it on the ground—right below the Thank You for Not Smoking sign. "Good for you."

Jessica bit her cheek. Connie Boyer didn't seem very interested. Maybe she didn't realize that Jessica was in the same movie and they were going to be working together. "I'm going to play one of your little sisters," she explained.

Connie sniffed.

Jessica squirmed. Connie wasn't being very receptive to her attempts to make conversation, but Jessica figured she'd probably been out late the night before at some fabulous Hollywood party.

"Do you know Johnny Buck?" Jessica couldn't resist asking.

"What is this, Twenty Questions? Don't you have something to do?" Connie asked irritably.

Jessica backed up. "I'm sorry," she said quickly. "I didn't mean to ask so many questions."

"Jacko!" Connie Boyer shouted. "Come over here and do something about this kid, would you?"

A young production assistant with wire-rimmed glasses and a scraggly beard scurried over and took Jessica by the arm. "Why don't you go over to the catering truck and see if they have any ice cream?" he suggested in a kind voice. He steered her firmly away from Connie.

Jessica felt her cheeks flushing bright red. They were treating her as if she were some kind of unauthorized pest or set crasher. "I wasn't doing anything!" she told Jacko.

Jacko pulled her behind a big camera and knelt down so that they were face-to-face. "I don't want to get into trouble, but take it from me—whatever she says, just say, 'Yes, Connie' and don't argue. If you do, she'll pull your ears off and feed them to her pet crocodile." With that, Jacko stood up and hurried across the soundstage, where someone else was calling his name.

Jessica blinked back tears. How had she managed to get off on the wrong foot like that? She'd just been sitting there minding her own business, and the next thing she knew, Jacko was giving her the same treatment the guy at the Chad's Burgers had given Steven.

Across the soundstage, she watched Connie conversing with Oliver. She appeared to be shouting. Oliver just nodded.

It looked as if he was on the receiving end of Connie's temper, just as Jessica had been. Jessica began to feel a little better. She shouldn't take it personally, she told herself. Connie Boyer was famous for being rude and obnoxious. It had made her a star.

But Connie hadn't always been a big star. She'd had to start at the bottom, like everyone else. She had paid her dues. Jessica was brand-new on the scene, just a kid. Why should Connie Boyer even give her the time of day?

Jessica would show Connie that she was a dedicated show business professional—just like Connie. Then Connie would be nice to her. Maybe she would even treat Jessica like a sister in real life. With Connie Boyer's help, Jessica would become a star too!

Elizabeth looked at her reflection in the makeup artist's mirror. It was her . . . but *more* her.

Every feature was exaggerated. Her lips. Her eyes. Her cheekbones. Even her dimple had been deepened with a little smudge of charcoal.

The makeup artist removed the large bib that protected Elizabeth's costume, a white velvet sailor suit.

"All right. Let's turn you over to one of the

assistant directors and let them do some lighting tests on this makeup. We may have to make some adjustments."

The makeup artist escorted Elizabeth out of the makeup and costume department and toward another of the huge buildings that made up the Filmworld studio complex.

Elizabeth and the makeup artist entered soundstage A through the enormous door. As soon as they walked in, Elizabeth could see people scurrying in every direction. Machinery whirred and hummed. Lights moved back and forth on metal tracks overhead. People seemed to be shouting instructions to each other from every corner of the cavernous room.

Elizabeth looked around, hoping to spot Jessica. But she didn't see her sister anywhere.

"Dave!" The makeup person flagged down one of the assistant directors. "This is Elizabeth Wakefield. She's ready for a test shoot on her makeup and costume."

Dave nodded and checked his clipboard. "OK. Got it. Come on, Elizabeth. Follow me."

Elizabeth hurried to keep up with Dave. He led her to a spot on the floor marked with some masking tape. "Stand right here while we get the lights set up. It'll probably take a while, so just relax."

Elizabeth did her best to relax, but it was hard when every three seconds somebody aimed a blinding light in her eyes.

When will I actually get to act? she wondered.

"Hold it!" a female voice bellowed. "Do I see what I think I see?"

The lights were shining in Elizabeth's eyes, and she couldn't see a thing. She could only hear voices.

"This is Elizabeth Wakefield," Dave said. "Is there a problem?"

"Is there a problem?" the female voice repeated sarcastically. "Yes, there is a problem. Do you realize that kid is wearing white?"

Elizabeth lifted her hand, trying to shield her eyes from the glare so that she could see who was so upset. It was really disconcerting to have somebody talking about her as though she weren't even there.

"The script calls for a white velvet suit," Dave explained.

"I don't care what the script says!" the female voice yelled. "I look awful in white. And I don't even want anybody in white standing near me in a scene. I look good in cream. Bone. Off-white. Put that kid in something off-white."

"Sailors don't wear off-white, Connie. They wear white," Dave pointed out in a reasonable tone.

Connie! Elizabeth stood up straighter. So the famous Connie Boyer had finally put in an appearance. Elizabeth was sorry she couldn't see her.

There was a long pause. Elizabeth could hear people whispering. Several more people clustered around, and the whispering grew more agitated. Finally another man began to talk.

"Connie, I understand how important this is to you, but the whole resolution of the story hinges on the suit being white. The story takes place during the Second World War. Your two little sisters are determined to be a part of the Navy USO show. The Navy dress uniforms are *white*. Remember how the scene is written? You're looking all over for your sisters. You don't see them at first because they've blended in with columns of sailors on parade. Then we get this spectacular close-up of you when you realize that—"

"Rewrite the script," Connie screamed. "Lose the Navy. Put 'em in the Army. I look good in green!"

Elizabeth heard a pair of high heels walk briskly away.

There was a long silence. Then . . . *clack* . . . *clack* . . . *clack* . . . the lights went out.

When the spots in front of Elizabeth's eyes cleared, nearly everyone was gone. The soundstage was practically deserted. The woman from makeup came over and took Elizabeth's arm with a heavy sigh. "I'll walk you over to wardrobe, hon."

"There's no mineral water in my trailer! If you don't get some mineral water in here in five minutes, you're fired!"

A harried-looking young woman came running out of Connie Boyer's personal trailer and bounded across the concrete lot toward the catering truck.

Elizabeth and Jessica hurried past her on their way back to soundstage A.

The girls had been reoutfitted in olive drab velvet Army uniforms. Jessica couldn't help feeling sorry about the change. After all, they didn't call it olive *drab* for nothing. Jessica pulled the brim of her hat down over her eyes and sighed. The white velvet had been so beautiful. And she'd never even had a chance to try it on. She'd just seen her outfit hanging in wardrobe with her name pinned to it.

Dave spotted the twins when they walked into the soundstage, and he came hurrying over. "Good. You look fine. Now, we've changed the script. Forget the Navy—you're now in the Army. And you're not on a boat, you're on an Army base. Come with me and I'll find somebody to run your revised lines with you." Dave settled them in some chairs and bounded away like a harried rabbit.

Behind them a woman worked at a long table. Script pages were spread out around her. She made notes on each page. Jacko brought her a cup of coffee and a sandwich and set it down at her elbow.

The woman looked up and smiled. "Thank you. Jacko, have those young ladies had any lunch?"

Jessica breathed a sigh of relief. Her stomach had been rumbling for the last hour, but after the way she'd been treated by Connie and Jacko, she'd been afraid even to mention food.

Jacko hurried over and grinned ruefully. "I'm so sorry. We've all been running in circles, and I forgot to ask you. What would you girls like for lunch?"

"How about tuna fish?" Jessica said.

"Roast beef, please," Elizabeth answered.

Jacko nodded. "I'll be back with sandwiches and sodas."

Jessica and Elizabeth smiled their thanks to the woman at the table. She smiled back and then bent over her work.

"So what do you think so far?" Jessica whispered.

"I think everybody's scared to death of Connie Boyer," Elizabeth whispered back. "And I don't blame them. She's a monster."

"She's not a monster," Jessica argued. "She's temperamental. And why shouldn't she be? She's a star."

"She's an illiterate miscreant," the lady at the table said, not bothering to whisper.

Jessica and Elizabeth both blinked in surprise.

"Allow me to introduce myself," the woman said with a smile. "I'm Harriet Hughes. The writer."

Eleven

"So when Filmworld bought your script," Elizabeth asked, "did you know Connie Boyer would be in it?"

Harriet swallowed her bite of sandwich and shook her head. "No. I had no idea." She picked up a plastic cup full of celery and olives and offered it to Elizabeth.

Elizabeth took a couple of olives and put them on her paper plate beside what was left of her sandwich.

Harriet had invited the girls to eat lunch with her. As far as Elizabeth was concerned, this was the most interesting thing that had happened to her so far that day. She loved meeting writers. And Harriet was really friendly and open, answering all of Elizabeth's questions.

"When a movie studio buys your script,"

Harriet explained, "you don't have any say over who's in the film. That's up to the studio."

"Were you glad when you heard that it was going to star Connie Boyer?" Jessica asked.

Harriet munched a potato chip. "I refuse to answer that question on the grounds that it might incriminate me."

"You don't like her, do you?" Elizabeth said, smiling.

"I don't like the way she treats people. But what offends me more is the way she treats people's work. She's fired more good writers from her television show than I can count. Then she butchers what they've written. If it works, she takes the credit. If it bombs, she says it's the writer's fault."

"But that's so unfair!" Elizabeth cried.

Harriet shrugged. "Welcome to show business."

"OK, girls," Dave said. "We're going to shoot a very short scene. It's the scene where Connie tells you that you have to get off the train and go to your grandmother's until the war is over. Do you know your lines?"

"They do," Harriet said. "We've been rehearsing together." She smiled at Elizabeth and Jessica. "When I wrote this story, you girls are exactly what I imagined."

Jessica smiled. "Thanks for telling me. I can use that." "I can use that" was something she heard actors say all the time on TV. It meant they would think about that piece of information while they were acting, and it would help them get into character.

The compliment made Jessica feel a little better about Harriet. Of course, Elizabeth was gaga over her because she was a writer. But Jessica thought Harriet had a lot of nerve criticizing Connie.

After all, Connie was the star of the movie. And of her TV show too. If she had to push a few writers around to get what she wanted . . . well, that's how you got to the top.

Elizabeth picked up her copy of the script. "Thank you," she said to Harriet.

"Don't be nervous," Dave told them as they walked out of the big soundstage, across a hall, and into another soundstage.

Jessica gasped when she saw the set. It was an old-fashioned train car with sleeping compartments, reproduced down to the last detail. Some assistants were moving large spotlights around. A mike dangling from a boom was being moved around over the set.

A woman hurried up to the twins and hastily powdered their faces while an assistant fluffed their hair and tweaked lint off their jackets.

On the other side of the large room, Connie Boyer conversed with Oliver in low tones.

"Look at Connie," Jessica whispered. "She looks gorgeous." Connie wore a trim 1940s Army uniform with a tightly fitted jacket and skirt. Her hair had been combed into a roll along the back of her head, and a soft wave fell over one eye.

Oliver clapped his hands. "OK, everybody. Let's try to shoot some film. Places."

Dave took Jessica and Elizabeth down to the car and placed them in one of the small sleeping compartments. "You stand here," he told Jessica, positioning her on one side of the train window. "Elizabeth, you stand at Connie's right elbow. I want you to move with her through the scene. You're trying to convince her not to leave you with your grandmother. You want to go with her, even if it means going overseas and being in danger."

Elizabeth nodded. "Got it."

A buzzer sounded.

People jumped out of the brightly lit stage area and into the shadows behind the cameras and lighting equipment.

Connie walked onto the set and lifted her chin. Immediately her assistant appeared with a mirror. Connie inspected her appearance with a critical eye, then dismissed the assistant with a curt nod.

"And . . . action!" Oliver shouted.

The cameras were rolling. The scene had started.

Connie reached up over the bunks and grabbed a suitcase. "You two are going to Grandma's," she said, dropping the suitcase on the lower bunk and opening the lid. She crossed the small sleeping compartment to the built-in dresser. Elizabeth crossed with her.

"Michelle, we don't want to go to Grandma's.

We want to go with you," Elizabeth argued.

"We want to serve our country," Jessica said. "Just like you do."

Connie took a pile of folded clothes from the drawer and crossed back to the suitcase. She dropped them in and patted them down. "Come on, girls. You know I can't take you with me. I would if I could. But I can't."

She started back toward the dresser. As Elizabeth hurried beside her she stepped on something that didn't feel like the floor.

"Watch it!" Connie snapped.

"Watch it"? I don't remember that line being in the script, Elizabeth thought.

"Cut!" Oliver yelled. "What happened?"

"She stepped on my toe," Connie said irritably.

Oliver stepped out of the darkness and onto the set. "We tried to get you to block the scene," he reminded Connie. "But you said you'd know what to do when the cameras started rolling."

"Are you saying it's my fault?" Connie demanded, her eyes blazing.

"I'm saying that we might want to walk through the scene a couple of times to make sure you don't zig when Elizabeth zags," he responded diplomatically.

"I'll zig whenever I darn well please," Connie snapped. "I want this scene rewritten. The problem is that there are too many people in this little sleeping compartment. That would never happen in real life."

"Somebody get Harriet, please," Oliver sighed.

Jessica stood a few feet behind Oliver. She'd just been written out of the scene. Harriet had argued, but Connie had insisted.

Jessica was determined not to get too angry at Connie. *Connie knows what she's doing,* she told herself sternly. *She said that my character doesn't really belong in the scene. She wouldn't be where she is today if she made bad decisions.*

She swallowed her anger. What was the point? There would be other scenes. She'd get her chance to show Connie what she could do.

Oliver took his position. "And . . . action!"

Connie reached up over the bunks and grabbed a suitcase. "You and your sister are going to Grandma's," she said, dropping the suitcase on the lower bunk and opening the lid. As she'd done before, she crossed over to the other side of the compartment to the built-in dresser. Elizabeth crossed with her.

"Michelle," Elizabeth argued, "I don't want to go to Grandma's. And I know Ramona doesn't either. We want to go with you and serve our country."

Connie took a pile of folded clothes from the drawer and crossed back to the suitcase. She dropped them in and patted them down. "You know I can't take you with me. I would if I could. But I can't."

Connie was supposed to turn right to go back to the dresser. But instead of turning right, she turned left and bumped right into Elizabeth.

Elizabeth tumbled backward. Her arm flew out

and hit the window. The plastic pane popped out and fell to the floor with a clatter. Then the whole wall of the train car toppled over with a crash.

"Cut!" Oliver shouted.

Elizabeth stood by Jessica, watching the tenth re-take of the scene. Now *she* had been written out. Connie had decided that the scene really belonged to her alone.

Oliver sighed. "And . . . action!"

Connie reached up over the bunks and grabbed a suitcase. She opened the lid and moved some of the clothes inside it around. "They won't like going to Grandma's while I go overseas with the USO show, but that's just tough." She slammed the suit-case shut.

"Cut! Print!" Oliver shouted. "That's a wrap. We got the shot. Thank you, everybody."

A buzzer sounded, signaling that the shoot was over.

Elizabeth turned to Jessica. "Well, I think that went well. Don't you?" she said dryly as they began trudging toward the exit.

"So we got written out of one scene," Jessica said lightly. "Big deal. So we got yelled at. Big deal. So we got pushed around. Big deal. Look on the bright side." She grinned. "At least we don't have to go to school. And we don't have any homework."

"Elizabeth! Jessica!" Dave hurried toward them, followed by another man in a Filmworld jacket.

The man was short and round. He wore glasses and had a long ponytail hanging out of the back of his baseball cap. "Here's somebody who's been dying to meet you," Dave said.

Elizabeth widened her eyes. Somebody actually *wanted* to talk to them?

"He looks like a rock promoter," Jessica whispered excitedly. She fluffed her hair.

"Girls, this is Mr. Blandon," Dave said warmly as the men came closer.

Elizabeth smiled as she shook Mr. Blandon's hand. He did look like some kind of promoter or producer. Maybe she and Jessica were doing better than she thought and had attracted some attention already.

"He's your on-set teacher," Dave continued. "One of the best in the business."

"Our . . . teacher?" Jessica repeated brokenly.

Mr. Blandon smiled. "I've spoken with all of your regular teachers and gotten copies of your textbooks. Don't you worry. I'll see to it that you don't miss one single test or assignment."

Twelve

"What do you mean, you haven't been in one scene yet?" Steven asked. "You've been going there every day for two weeks. What have you been doing?" Steven was over his cold and was dressed for school.

"Math," Jessica answered resentfully. "And lots of it. Mr. Blandon is a math fiend! And an English addict. And his favorite thing is tests. I've done more homework in the last two weeks than I usually do in two months!"

Steven looked over at Elizabeth. "Is she telling the truth?"

They were sitting at the breakfast table together for the first time since Elizabeth and Jessica had started on the movie. The script was undergoing yet another rewrite, so the girls didn't have to report as early as they usually did. Most days they left the house long before Steven got up and came home after he had gone to bed.

"She's telling the truth," Elizabeth said. "Connie Boyer takes up most of every day arguing with the director and everybody else."

"She's not *arguing*," Jessica protested. "She's trying to make the movie the best it can be."

Elizabeth rolled her eyes. "Admit it, Jess. Connie's exactly what Harriet said she is: a know-nothing."

"She's a star!" Jessica insisted stubbornly. "And it's not her fault Harriet can't rewrite fast enough." A little part of Jessica was finding it harder and harder to defend Connie. But she was sure that when the film was in the can and Connie realized what a great actress Jessica really was, she would quit treating the twins with such contempt.

"There's a lot of down time while Harriet rewrites," Elizabeth explained to Steven. "When they don't need us on the set, we're supposed to report to Mr. Blandon."

"And if we don't report to him," Jessica complained bitterly, "he comes looking for us. Yesterday I got Jacko to hide me behind the catering truck. But Mr. Blandon found me. The man has the soul of a bloodhound." She set her spoon down in her cereal bowl with a clatter. "And you! You're supposed to be our personal manager," she reminded him in an accusatory voice. "You should do something."

Elizabeth laughed. "There's nothing anybody can do. The law and the unions are really strict about on-set teaching. Mr. Blandon has to keep a record of the time he spends with us and the amount of homework he gives us."

"Which is more than the law should allow." Jessica groaned. "Well, anyway, it is *so* nice to be able to sleep late."

"Late?" Steven exclaimed. "You used to complain that this was the crack of dawn."

Jessica popped a strawberry in her mouth. "I know. But now that I really *do* have to get up at the crack of dawn, I appreciate the comfort of my former life."

"We'll be getting back to our former life soon," Elizabeth reminded her.

"No, we won't," Jessica argued. "Pretty soon we're going to get our chance to show everyone at Filmworld that we can act. And we're going to knock 'em dead. We'll be the toast of Hollywood." She held up two fingers and pressed them close together. "And me and Connie Boyer are going to be like that! Best friends."

Steven snapped his fingers. "Speaking of best friends, I saw a bunch of Unicorns in the mall the other day. They all said to tell you hello and wanted to know if you would be at the big game."

Jessica felt a little stab of envy. Most of the middle school went to Sweet Valley High's annual basketball game against Big Mesa. She could just see all the Unicorns sitting in the stands, talking in loud voices about how they knew Steven Wakefield *personally*.

Jessica clenched her jaw. Steven was *her* big brother. If anybody was going to bask in his reflected glory, it ought to be her and Elizabeth.

"The other guys on the team are pretty blown away that you two are in a movie with Connie Boyer," Steven went on. "They all wanted to know if you would be coming to the game. I think they want to ask you a bunch of questions about Connie Boyer. But I told everybody you guys usually don't get home until late." He pushed his chair back with a squeak. "Oh, well. See you later."

Steven left the kitchen, and Jessica stared gloomily across the table at Elizabeth. "I don't believe this! The high-school basketball team actually *wants* us at one of their parties—and we're not going to be able to go."

"Cheer up," Elizabeth said lightly. "You won't care about high-school parties when you're the toast of Hollywood."

The toast of Hollywood, Jessica repeated to herself. She knew she should be feeling glamorous and important, but somehow, toast or no toast, she *did* care about missing a chance to see her friends. A lump rose in her throat, and hot tears stung her eyes. She missed the Unicorns—even Lila. She wanted to go to the game and tell people she was Steven Wakefield's little sister. She wanted to go to the party after the game.

She still wanted to be the toast of Hollywood. But she wouldn't mind being the toast of Sweet Valley too.

Mr. Wakefield came into the kitchen, straightening his tie. "Girls," he announced in a comic English accent, "your limousine is here."

Jessica dropped her head on her arms and groaned unhappily.

"Did I miss something?" Mr. Wakefield asked with surprise.

Elizabeth laughed. "Come on, Jessica. Dave said today's the day we start shooting the big dance number."

"He's been saying that for the last three days," Jessica pointed out.

Elizabeth dropped her napkin. "I know. But let's think positive."

Jessica sighed. "We might as well. What choice do we have?"

"Kick . . . step . . . kick . . . step . . . that's it!" The choreographer clapped her hands, applauding the twins. "I'll tell Oliver you're ready whenever he is."

The choreographer left the set. And for the first time since filming had started, Elizabeth felt as though she was part of something special. They were going to dance—all three of them, Jessica, Elizabeth, and Connie. They were going to sing too, and the twins had spent the morning warming up with the vocal coach.

"I like these costumes," Jessica said.

"Me too." They wore khaki tights, white T-shirts, and combat boots. It was a cute dance number set in the barracks of an Army base.

Moments later Connie arrived in an identical outfit. She didn't even bother to say hello before she began to stretch. Elizabeth wondered if they should say anything, then decided not to.

Oliver came over holding a cup of coffee. "Ready for the dance number? Remember, I want big movement, OK?"

Elizabeth smiled and nodded.

Oliver walked back and took his place next to the camera. "Sing it the way you rehearsed it, but don't worry too much about the notes. You'll overdub the singing in postproduction." He turned to the set pianist. "Give us a music cue, please."

The pianist played a short intro, and Oliver pointed his finger, signaling Connie and the twins to begin.

For once it looked as though Connie had come prepared. She knew the combination perfectly, and every movement was precisely on the beat. She knew all the words to the song too. And she had a strong voice.

Elizabeth pivoted and crossed behind her.

Jessica moved in a circle.

Connie extended her leg. Jessica caught her toe, then pushed, sending Connie into a spin.

Elizabeth danced as she had never danced before. She felt graceful and athletic. The three of them danced so well as a team, it gave her goose bumps.

The music came to an end. As rehearsed, Connie went down on one knee, Elizabeth sat on her other knee, and Jessica leaned on Connie's shoulder.

"Cut!" Oliver shouted. "Perfect! That was great!"

Connie stood up abruptly, and Elizabeth tumbled off her knee. "I don't like it."

"What do you mean, you don't like it?" Oliver asked.

Connie put her hands on her hips and strode back and forth across the set, eyeing Elizabeth and Jessica.

"Something's been bothering me about these girls, and I've finally figured out what it is." She pointed dramatically. "They're too blond. I should be the only blonde in the scene. Their blondness undercuts the drama of my blondness."

"But I don't want to be a brunette!" Jessica protested.

The hairdresser pressed a pedal, and Jessica's chair tilted back so that her head was poised over the sink. "It's just a rinse, sweetie. It'll wash out in a few weeks."

An hour later, on her way back to the set, Elizabeth passed a mirror and did a double take. It was hard to get used to her new look. She decided it was a good thing she wasn't a natural brunette. The brown hair made her look naturally hideous.

"Where's Dave?" Elizabeth asked Jacko as he positioned her and Jessica on the set.

"He quit," Jacko said. "He said he couldn't take it anymore. Connie's assistant quit too." When Jacko was satisfied that they were standing in the right spot, he hurried off the set.

Connie stalked onto the set, ran a critical eye over their hair, and then nodded as if she was satisfied. "OK. Let's do it again."

Oliver stood in the shadows whispering with a tall man. "That's Mr. Libby, the executive producer," Jessica whispered to Elizabeth. "I met him the first day."

Elizabeth stood up a little straighter. If the executive producer was going to be watching, she wanted to make a good impression.

Oliver walked over to his director's chair. "Folks, we're running behind, and that means we're running over budget. So let's try to get this in as few takes as possible. Music cue, please."

The piano music began, and Elizabeth, Jessica, and Connie launched into the dance number. Once again it went like clockwork. Elizabeth felt as if she had been dancing the combination her whole life. Before she knew it, it was over, and she was sitting on Connie's knee.

"Cut! Print!" Oliver shouted.

"Not so fast!" Connie said. "These two are upstaging me again."

Elizabeth's heart began to sink into her stomach.

She was beginning to think Connie Boyer wasn't just rude and obnoxious, she was *insane!* No matter what they did, she accused them of upstaging her.

Next thing you know, Elizabeth thought sourly, *she'll think we're upstaging her just by* breathing.

Jessica and Elizabeth sipped sodas while Oliver, Connie, Carla, Harriet, and Mr. Libby argued. The argument had been going on for twenty minutes.

Elizabeth held up two fingers and pressed them together. "When you and Connie are *like that,* you might want to talk to her about this upstaging obsession," she told Jessica.

Jessica was about to reply when suddenly Connie screamed, "That's the way I want it. So that's the way it's going to be!"

"Game over," Elizabeth said, slurping her soda through a straw.

Oliver walked toward the girls with a shuffling gate. He looked exhausted, like a man who had just gone three rounds with an alligator. "Girls, we've made a few changes and . . . um . . ." Oliver swallowed and refused to meet their eyes. "We've decided the number works best as a solo for Connie."

Elizabeth closed her eyes and moaned. "So what do you want us to do now?"

Oliver sighed. "I'm not sure yet. So you might as well report to Mr. Blandon. I'm sure he'll have something to keep you busy."

Jessica crumpled her can in her fist, wishing it

were Connie Boyer's neck. This was the last straw. The very last straw. She'd made all the excuses she could for Connie Boyer. She could put up with being treated like a pest. She could put up with being written out of scenes. She could even put up with having to dye her hair. But *this* was too much!

Jessica wouldn't be Connie Boyer's friend even if she *begged* her.

Steven got off the bus and quickly walked two blocks to the entrance gate of Filmworld. The security guard was a pretty intimidating-looking guy—bigger than the guy who'd thrown him out of the Chad's Burgers. Steven sighed. He sure didn't want to take another exploratory dive into the world of garbage.

But it had been pretty obvious to Steven that morning that his sisters were miserable, and it was up to him to do something about it. He was their brother. More important, he was their manager. He had a duty to protect their interests . . . and his own. If they weren't happy, they wouldn't perform well. And if they didn't perform well, they wouldn't become big stars.

There was a car at stake. And a ski condo, if he remembered the offer correctly.

He straightened the lapels on his sport coat and hoped his sunglasses didn't look as cheap as they really were.

"Can I help you?" the guard asked as Steven approached the gate.

"I'm Steven Wakefield. I'm here to visit two of my clients."

The security guard raised his eyebrows. "The executives are getting younger every day." He reached for his cell phone and began punching buttons with his thumb. "What did you say your name was?"

"Steven Wakefield. And my clients are Elizabeth and Jessica Wakefield."

When Elizabeth came out of the ladies' room, an assistant director hurried past her on his way to the other side of the soundstage, where Connie and Oliver were having a script conference. "Steven Wakefield?" he barked into his cell phone. "Never heard of him!"

"Steven Wakefield!" Elizabeth cried. "That's our brother."

But the assistant director apparently couldn't hear her, since Connie Boyer was screaming, "And furthermore, if it weren't for me, this lousy picture wouldn't even be getting made, so . . ."

"Elizabeth!" A firm hand closed over her upper arm. It was Mr. Blandon. "You're late to class," he said firmly. "And we've got a lot of math problems to complete."

"But—"

"No buts," Mr. Blandon said cheerily, pulling her out of the soundstage and down the hallway toward his classroom. "Someday you'll thank me," he promised. "Because no matter how big a star you become, you'll need to be able to read and write and think logically."

"Unless you're Connie Boyer," Elizabeth couldn't resist muttering.

The security guard lowered the phone from his ear. "Sorry. I can't get you in. But it was a nice try."

Steven sighed. Some way to treat a manager.

He walked to the corner, eyeing the high chain-link fence. There had to be a way to get in. And once he got in, he'd find the director and tell him that two of his stars were very unhappy. Then Steven would offer to negotiate a deal—a deal that would include a limo ride to the Sweet Valley High–Big Mesa game and the after-game party for his sisters . . . and their manager. That ought to bring their morale up, he figured.

At that moment a Pizza Heaven delivery wagon came slowly around the corner. Behind the wheel was Jerry Plister, who just happened to be a senior forward on the Sweet Valley High basketball team.

Steven waved the truck over.

"Wakefield!" Jerry said with a grin. "What are you doing here?"

"Funny you should ask," Steven said. "I was looking for a job delivering pizza."

Thirteen

"Girls! Oliver wants you right away!" Jacko stood in the doorway of the classroom and beckoned.

Yes! Jessica thought happily. Mr. Blandon was in the process of assigning a two-page essay on the causes of the American Revolution. Personally, Jessica had a big problem with the whole school-on-the-set concept. And any activity, even standing around watching Connie Boyer scream, was better than writing an essay.

Mr. Blandon closed his book. "I know you girls are disappointed that we can't work on our essays now. But we'll do them later, I promise."

Jacko tapped his foot. "I hate to hurry you, but come *on*."

Jessica grabbed her little Army hat, and she and

Elizabeth scrambled up out of their seats. "What's going on?" Jessica asked.

"Connie's just found out she's going to be on the cover of *Vanity Galore*. She's so thrilled, she's actually smiling. Oliver wants to take advantage of her good mood while it lasts. He wants to shoot the scene in the hospital."

"All right!" Jessica cried. "That's my biggest scene."

"Jacko," Elizabeth said as they hurried down the corridor, "I think our brother may be somewhere in the complex. His name is Steven. Could you see about getting him in?"

"Sure thing," Jacko said absently. "Just as soon as we get the scene going."

The three of them hurried into soundstage C, which had been set up to look like a military hospital.

Connie Boyer was already on the set. She lay in a hospital bed with a bandage around her head. Even though she was supposed to be seriously wounded, her makeup was perfect and her cheeks were a rosy pink.

She and Oliver were discussing the scene while technical people moved lights and booms around. A swarm of people from makeup descended on the twins, powdering, teasing, painting, blotting, and spraying.

When Oliver shouted "Ready," somebody blasted Jessica's hair with a last shot of hair spray, and then the swarm of makeup artists disappeared into the maze of cameras, wires, lights, booms, and cranes.

Jessica took her place at Connie's bedside. Elizabeth hovered at the foot of the bed.

Connie fluttered her eyelids, as if she were very weak. Her lips parted slightly. She was getting into character, Jessica thought admiringly. With great effort, Connie lifted her hand for Jessica to take, and her lips moved faintly, as if she wanted to say something. Jessica bent closer to catch her words. "Don't block my shot," Connie whispered, "or I'll scream the place down."

"Action!" Oliver shouted.

Connie let her head roll toward Jessica.

Jessica closed her eyes and squeezed them shut. It was hard having to get into character on a moment's notice. She tried to think of something really, *really* sad, but it wasn't coming.

She felt Connie's hand begin to tighten around hers.

Jessica let her lips tremble, trying to buy a little time. She was supposed to sound heartbroken. Her opening line was, "Please don't die, Michelle."

My sister is injured, she told herself. *Maybe even dying*.

Jessica could feel the tension on the set building. She could feel Oliver waiting for her to launch into her lines. She could feel Elizabeth growing nervous.

Then she felt Connie's hand grip hers like a vise. Jessica let out a shrill cry of pain. "*Pleaaseeeee* don't die!" she shrieked.

Connie released her hand.

Jessica wasn't too happy about being rushed, but she'd heard Oliver say time was money. "We don't have an act without you," she said in her most wistful voice. She gazed at Connie. "Ramona and I need you. So do your fans."

Connie fluttered her eyelids. "I'm sorry, sweetheart," she said in a faint voice. "I feel like I'm letting you down."

Elizabeth leaned forward. "You could *never* let us down," she said, a sob in her voice.

Connie sat straight up in the bed like a jackknife. Jessica and Elizabeth both jumped back.

Jessica couldn't help thinking that for somebody who was supposed to be dying, Connie sure was spry.

"Cut!" Oliver yelled. "What's the matter, Connie?"

"They're both leaning into the camera," Connie complained. "They're obscuring my profile."

"Girls, don't lean over Connie. Let's do it again."

Connie lay back down. Jessica took her hand, and Elizabeth positioned herself at the foot of the bed. Connie glared at Jessica. "And don't take all day to start the scene this time."

"Action!"

Jessica tried to make her eyes look large and sad. "Please don't die," she pleaded softly. "We don't have an act without you. Ramona and I need you. So do your fans."

Connie fluttered her eyelids. "I'm sorry, sweetheart," she said in a faint voice. "I feel like I'm letting you . . ." She sat back up. "Oliver! I know what's bugging me—their eyes. Those blue-green eyes are too dramatic with the dark hair. They'll steal the scene. Fit them with brown tinted contacts!"

Jessica dropped Connie's hand. "No!" she protested. By the time Connie got through with them, their own mother wouldn't recognize them in the movie, much less the Unicorns and the big-wigs in Hollywood.

Connie sat up. "Nobody tells *me* no, kid!"

"Stop calling me kid!" Jessica retorted.

Connie's mouth fell open. Jessica knew she was in for a screaming session. But she didn't care. She'd scream right back!

Before anyone could say a word, Jessica heard a scuffling sound, and then the sound of voices raised in an argument.

"Hey! Who are you?" a man demanded.

"I'm Elizabeth and Jessica Wakefield's personal manager! So take your hands off—*hey!* Who do you think you're shoving?" Steven shouted.

"Stop!" Jessica yelled. "That's my brother!" Without thinking, she jumped on Connie's bed, stepped over her body, and jumped off the other side of the bed. She was determined to get to the door of the soundstage before the guards could hurt Steven.

Connie let out an outraged yell.

But Jessica didn't care. *Let Connie yell*, she thought as she hurried over to Steven. *She's better at yelling than she is at acting anyway.*

Elizabeth ran behind Jessica. "Stop!" she shouted to the security guards. "That's our brother!"

Two security guards were dragging a pizza delivery boy toward the exit. They stopped and turned Steven around so the twins could get a good look at him. "This guy?"

"That guy," Elizabeth confirmed.

"You sure?" one of the guards asked.

"Yes," Elizabeth insisted. "That's Steven Wakefield. He's our brother."

Steven twisted out of the security guards' grasp. He tugged at the hem of his red-and-green striped polyester shirt and straightened his spinning-pizza beanie. "I also happen to be their personal manager."

Oliver came running over. With him was Mr. Libby.

"What's the problem?" Oliver asked, his eyes darting around the assembled group. "What's going on here?"

Steven stepped forward. "The problem is that my clients are not being treated with the respect they deserve."

Oliver rolled his eyes. "Look, kid. I got big problems right now, and—"

"And that's why you should probably talk to me," Mr. Libby broke in, putting his arm over Steven's shoulders. "I'm Wallace Libby, the executive producer. Let's all go in my office and talk."

"I'm sorry," Mr. Libby said. "But there's absolutely nothing I can do about Connie Boyer. Or the amount of screen time your sisters—*clients*," he amended, "receive." He smiled ruefully. "You see, Ms. Boyer owns fifty-one percent of this production. When she moved from television to movies, the only roles she could get were in horror films. She wanted to expand to other genres, but she had no luck. So she decided to create a movie project for herself."

"Well, it's no surprise about the horror films," Elizabeth said. "She's horrible!"

"And mean," Jessica added.

"If it's any consolation," Mr. Libby said, "she's mean to me too. Why do you think I spend most of my time in here instead of out there?"

Jessica took off her Army hat and threw it on the ground. "Then I think I speak for both of us when I say I quit."

Elizabeth gasped. "Jess! You mean you're walking away from a *movie* role?"

Steven smiled. If Jessica had the guts to quit, that improved their negotiating position one hundred percent. He wished he hadn't taken his sunglasses off when he put on the pizza delivery outfit. If he was going to be a Hollywood power broker, he ought to look the part.

Mr. Libby reached into his desk drawer, removed a file, and handed it to Steven. "Please advise your clients that they can't quit without being in breach of contract."

"Oh." *So much for that.* But Steven was determined to get at least one concession for his clients.

"Well . . . can't you at least reduce the amount of homework they have to do?"

Mr. Libby shook his head. "Sorry. That's out of my hands too."

Steven stood up and pounded the table until the plastic pizza on his beanie began to spin. "This is an outrage. You're holding them prisoner. Subjecting them to abuse. Depriving them of their friends and family. Making them wear weird makeup. That's . . . that's . . . that's . . ."

"That's show business," Mr. Libby finished for him.

"I'm sorry," Steven told the girls as they walked him to the entrance. "I'm not much of a manager."

"Maybe not," Elizabeth said. "But thanks for trying." She gave him an unhappy smile.

"Yeah," Jessica said. "You may be lousy as a manager, but you're OK for a big brother."

Steven walked out of the gate and lifted his hand, waving good-bye. The security guard closed the gate behind him and stood with his arms crossed, watching Steven go.

The twins waved at him from the other side of the chain-link fence.

Steven sighed. Normally, of course, seeing the twins locked up and away from him would have been a dream come true. But he'd seen firsthand what they were going through. It was hard not to feel sorry for them.

And what would happen to his ski condo if the few times his clients actually got to appear on-screen they weren't even allowed to look like themselves?

"I want this whole scene rewritten from top to bottom," Connie yelled.

Elizabeth and Jessica sat side by side in folding canvas chairs while Connie paced back and forth, raging at Oliver.

Elizabeth kept thinking about Steven. She hoped he didn't feel too bad about what had happened.

"I want them out of the scene altogether," Connie raged on. "It'll work a lot better if it's just me and a doctor."

"What if we behaved just as rudely to her as she does to us?" Jessica whispered. "She'd fire us, right?"

"Maybe," Elizabeth answered, "maybe not. She might keep us here just so she could torture us. Besides, you know how Mom and Dad are about us finishing what we start."

"Hmpf," Jessica muttered. "And I bet that if I got fired for being rude to a grown-up—even Connie Boyer—they'd probably ground me. Talk about a lose-lose situation!"

"Well?" Connie screamed at Oliver. "What are you waiting for? Let's get started on the rewrite."

Oliver turned to one of his assistants. "Would you please get Harriet?" he asked. His voice was polite. Very, *very* polite. It was the voice of a man whose patience had been tried to the very limits of human endurance.

When he saw Jessica and Elizabeth looking at him, he smiled at the girls—a big gargoyle grin complete with clenched teeth. "Why don't you two go see what Mr. Blandon has for you to do?"

Elizabeth and Jessica didn't even bother to answer. They just got up and trudged across the soundstage.

Harriet came hurrying up to them. She smiled and winked at Elizabeth. "Hi. I just talked to Mr. Blandon. I suggested that instead of an essay, you girls might like to script a scene for yourselves. I don't know that we can actually use it, but if you want, I'll go over it with you and give you some scriptwriting tips."

Elizabeth's heart lifted. Harriet Hughes seemed to be the only person on the whole set who cared about the twins enough to try to do something to relieve the misery of their situation. "Thanks!" she said in a heartfelt voice. "Thanks a million."

"Anything for a fellow writer," Harriet answered with a smile.

"Do you realize I haven't talked to one Unicorn in over two weeks?" Jessica said as the girls climbed the stairs to their rooms that night.

"I haven't talked to Amy or Maria either," Elizabeth said. "I really wonder what's going on at school. Don't you?"

"I know what's going on. Everybody's getting

ready to have a great time at the Sweet Valley High game tomorrow night. And at the party afterward. But *we'll* probably be sitting around that stupid soundstage doing homework or listening to Connie Boyer scream." A tear trickled down Jessica's cheek.

After Steven had left, things had gone from bad to worse. Connie really had it in for Jessica now. Every single time Jessica moved or opened her mouth in a scene, Connie complained that Jessica was upstaging her. Or overacting. Or leaning into her shot. Or getting in her way.

Steven's door was closed. Jessica guessed he was already asleep, resting up for the next day.

Jessica went into her room and sat down on her bed. The tears were coming faster now. All Jessica wanted in the world was to go to the game and watch her big brother play and then go to the after-game party with the rest of her friends.

Suddenly the bathroom door flew open.

"I have an idea!" Elizabeth announced breathlessly. "We owe Louise and Tammy Parker a dirty trick. I think it's time we evened things up. Starting now."

Jessica looked at the clock. "How can we play a dirty trick this late at night? Dirty tricks are complicated. They take planning. They take props. They take time."

"All we need for this one is a phone book," Elizabeth said with a smile.

Fourteen

"She's doing it again!" Connie screamed. "They're both doing it! Upstaging me!"

Finally! Elizabeth thought with relief. Her hair was wet with sweat from the hot lights. They'd been working on this scene for over two hours, and Elizabeth had been wondering when Connie would start screaming about being upstaged.

"I want this scene rewritten," Connie yelled. "Oliver!"

"Harriet!" Oliver shouted.

"I'm here!" Harriet called out from behind a camera. She stepped forward into the light. "Connie, I don't think the problem is the way the scene is written." Harriet began circling the twins, eyeing them. "Nope. It's not the writing that's the problem." She stepped closer to Connie. "It's them. The twins."

"Huh?" Connie's eyes darted toward them.

"I agree one hundred percent. They're upstaging you," Harriet said.

Elizabeth gasped. "We are not! How can you say that?"

Jessica threw up her hands. "I thought we were here to act! If you don't want us to act, what do you want us to do?"

Elizabeth gazed at Harriet with hurt eyes. "I thought . . . I thought you were on our side," she finished in a small voice.

"I'm on the side of the movie," Harriet said firmly. "The story won't work if the star's not the focus of the audience's attention. Connie's right. You're upstaging her—because you're just too cute."

Jessica turned to Elizabeth. "See that? She's selling us out! I don't *believe* this."

"Now, girls . . . ," Oliver began.

"Kids are just natural scene stealers," Harriet went on. "I think we should seriously consider replacing them with older girls. Older girls just won't be as appealing on-screen."

Connie smiled. "Harriet, that's the first good idea you've had since we started this movie." She walked over to Elizabeth and Jessica. "You're fired," she said shortly.

Jessica's hands flew to her face, and she burst into tears.

Elizabeth's lip trembled. "But we want to be in the movie," she cried in a pitiful voice.

"I'll go call Star Quality and see if they can send us replacements this afternoon." Harriet walked past Elizabeth and Jessica as if they had never existed.

Oliver sank down into his director's chair, his shoulders slumped. He raked his fingers through his thin hair. When he spoke, his voice sounded strained. "Girls, please go to Mr. Libby's office and . . . and . . . tell him Ms. Boyer has requested that you be terminated." Oliver shook his head wearily. "I've got to get a real job," he muttered. "Something low-stress—like stunt driving."

Elizabeth took Jessica's arm. "Come on, Jessica," she said, weeping. "We might as well go on home. We're fired."

Jessica let out a loud wail followed by a hiccuping sob. "It's so unfair."

"Tough break," Elizabeth heard Jacko whisper as they made their way through the silent crowd of camera operators and lighting techs.

Jessica stopped. She lifted her face and stared off at a point somewhere in space. "You can chew us up and spit us out," she said in a dramatic voice, "but you can't crush our spirit. Nothing you do to us can take away our talent . . . or our hope . . . or our—*ouch!*" She turned to glare at Elizabeth, who had pinched her twin's arm.

"You made your point," Elizabeth hissed. "Now

let's get out of here before they feel so bad they change their minds."

On their way out they had to pass Harriet, who was speaking to someone on a cell phone. "Yes. The Parker twins? I'm very familiar with their work . . . mmm-hmmm . . ."

Elizabeth lifted her head and looked Harriet right in the eye.

Harriet winked.

Elizabeth winked back. *Lucky for us*, she thought, *Harriet is in the phone book.*

"Come *on*, Elizabeth!" Jessica shouted. "We're going to be late."

For once Jessica was ready before Elizabeth. She was even ready before Steven, who was still in his room getting his gear together.

Elizabeth stuck her head out of her room. "What's the hurry?"

"I haven't seen my friends in over two weeks," Jessica explained. "I want to get there early so I can save enough seats for everybody."

Steven came out of his room with his athletic bag. "I'm sorry you guys got fired. But I'm glad you got fired in time to see the game."

"Me too." Jessica had talked Mr. and Mrs. Wakefield into a shopping spree that afternoon, and she was all dressed up for the occasion in new flared red denim jeans, a matching jacket, and lug-soled sneakers.

And she wasn't wearing any makeup. She'd worn enough makeup over the last two weeks to last her for a while.

Elizabeth came out of her room in a new blue cotton skirt and a matching sweater with a lace collar.

Steven led the way down the steps.

"Mom! Dad!" Jessica shouted. "We're ready."

"Oh, they've already left," Steven announced.

Jessica frowned. "So how are we getting to the game?"

Steven opened the door, peeked out, and grinned. "Ah! Good! Right on time." He removed his sunglasses from his bag and put them on. "As your personal manager, I negotiated a couple of severance perks."

"Like what?" Jessica asked with a giggle.

Steven pointed to the street with his thumb. "Like that."

Jessica looked outside and let out a shriek of joy.

Parked at the curb was their long black studio limo. And inside it were Lila Fowler, Janet Howell, Mandy Miller, Tamara Chase, Kimberly Haver, Ellen Riteman, Maria Hughes, and Amy Sutton.

"Steven!" Elizabeth gasped. "How did you . . ."

Steven grinned. "Mr. Libby called and asked if there was anything that might make you guys feel better about what happened." Steven laughed. "I suggested that he give you and your personal manager a night of star treatment. After the game, the limo's taking us all to the party. And after the party,

you and the Unicorns and some other kids from
school are going with me and the rest of the team
to Teen Trend, a club in Hollywood."

"All right, Steven!" Jessica lifted her hand and
smacked her brother a high five. "You are a *great*
manager."

"And a great brother," Elizabeth added.
"Right, Jessica?"

"Right!" Jessica agreed. "But don't expect that
XT-540 anytime soon," she said before ducking into
the limo to join her friends.

"That movie was *awful!*" Jessica said as she and
Elizabeth walked out of the movie theater.

Elizabeth nodded. "I can see why it got such bad
reviews. I don't think we missed much by not
being in it."

Jessica laughed. "No. And where were Tammy
and Louise? I mean, their names were in the credits, but I never saw one glimpse of them."

"Their scenes probably wound up on the cutting
room floor," Elizabeth answered. "Connie probably
thought they upstaged her too. So she just cut out
the part of the little sisters altogether."

It had been several months since their movie ad-
venture, but Mr. Libby had tried to make it up to
them. He had paid them triple scale for the days
they had worked—which had added up to a lot of
shopping sprees.

They'd gotten something else out of it too.

A girl walking out of another movie gave Jessica a long and envious look. "Great outfit," she said.

"Thanks!" Jessica smiled and ran her hand over the plush fabric of her white velvet sailor suit.

"Hey, look! There's Cammi Adams coming out of cinema four." Elizabeth lifted her hand and waved.

"I didn't know Cammi Adams ever left the library," Jessica said under her breath. "Talk about a study grind!"

"Cammi does study a lot," Elizabeth said. "But she's really nice."

"If you say so," Jessica said skeptically. "Personally, I can't relate to anyone who does extra math problems for *fun*."

Does Cammi care about anything besides studying? Find out in Sweet Valley Twins *#108,* **CAMMI'S CRUSH.**

Bantam Books in the SWEET VALLEY TWINS series.
Ask your bookseller for the books you have missed.

SIGN UP FOR THE SWEET VALLEY HIGH® FAN CLUB!

Hey, girls! Get all the gossip on Sweet Valley High's® most popular teenagers when you join our fantastic Fan Club! As a member, you'll get all of this really cool stuff:

- Membership Card with your own personal Fan Club ID number
- A Sweet Valley High® Secret Treasure Box
- Sweet Valley High® Stationery
- Official Fan Club Pencil (for secret note writing!)
- Three Bookmarks
- A "Members Only" Door Hanger
- Two Skeins of J. & P. Coats® Embroidery Floss with flower barrette instruction leaflet
- Two editions of *The Oracle* newsletter
- Plus exclusive Sweet Valley High® product offers, special savings, contests, and much more!

Be the first to find out what Jessica & Elizabeth Wakefield are up to by joining the Sweet Valley High® Fan Club for the one-year membership fee of only $6.25 each for U.S. residents, $8.25 for Canadian residents (U.S. currency). Includes shipping & handling.

Send a check or money order (do not send cash) made payable to "Sweet Valley High® Fan Club" along with this form to:

SWEET VALLEY HIGH® FAN CLUB, BOX 3919-B, SCHAUMBURG, IL 60168-3919

NAME _____
(Please print clearly)

ADDRESS _____

CITY _____ STATE _____ ZIP _____
(Required)

AGE _____ BIRTHDAY _____ / _____ / _____